"You don't trust anyone with your heart?"

The question was so smooth and gentle Chloe was taken aback. She answered sadly as if to herself. "No."

"I had a very bleak childhood." Gabriel empathized with her. "All I could ever think was run, run, run, but I stayed for my mother's sake."

Chloe was stunned by the revelation. "Gabriel, I'm so sorry." A tremendous sympathy flowered from her body.

"Gracious lady." His voice sounded both tender and a little scathing. He glanced at her. How beautiful. He had craved beauty all his life, yet something about her made his heart throb painfully. It had from that very first day when she walked into his office. "No need to be, Chloe." He spoke dismissively. "It might have been a struggle, but it made me tough." His rugged face was dark and shadowed. "I know the toughness bothers you."

Chloe couldn't answer. There was no way to deny it, but, tenderhearted, she sensed she had wounded him.

Dear Reader,

Remember the magic of the film *It's a Wonderful Life*? The warmth and tender emotion of *Truly, Madly, Deeply*? The feel-good humor of *Heaven Can Wait*?

Well, we can't promise you Alan Rickman or Warren Beatty, but we know you'll be delighted with the latest miniseries in Harlequin Romance®: **GUARDIAN ANGELS**. It brings together all of your favorite ingredients for a perfect novel: great heroes, feisty heroines, breathtaking romance, all with a celestial spin. Written by four of our star authors, this witty and wonderful series features four real-life angels—all of whom are perfect advertisements for heaven!

Already available are *The Boss, the Baby and the Bride* by Day Leclaire, *Heavenly Husband* by Carolyn Greene and *A Groom for Gwen* by Jeanne Allan. This month it's the turn of popular Australian author Margaret Way with *Gabriel's Mission*. This is an emotional story that sees Chloe taking one risk too many and, before she knows it, her boss is close by her side.

Have a heavenly read!

The Editors

Falling in love sometimes needs a little help from above!

GUARDIAN ANGELS

Margaret Way
Gabriel's Mission

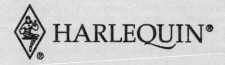

HARLEQUIN®

TORONTO • NEW YORK • LONDON
AMSTERDAM • PARIS • SYDNEY • HAMBURG
STOCKHOLM • ATHENS • TOKYO • MILAN • MADRID
PRAGUE • WARSAW • BUDAPEST • AUCKLAND

ISBN 0-373-03532-2

GABRIEL'S MISSION

First North American Publication 1998.

Copyright © 1998 by Margaret Way, Pty., Ltd.

This edition published by arrangement with Harlequin Books S.A.

® and TM are trademarks of the publisher. Trademarks indicated with ® are registered in the United States Patent and Trademark Office, the Canadian Trade Marks Office and in other countries.

Printed in U.S.A.

PROLOGUE

HEAVEN

TITUS and Thomas came tumbling down the grass, rolling ecstatically across the cushiony emerald sward, hurtling onwards to the stream that flashed silver in the all-pervading shining light. They often played this tumbling game. They loved it. Rolling from the very top of the undulating hill with its thick sprinkling of wildflowers, into the translucent water below. With their wings tucked back they dived to the bottom where gorgeous little fish, lovely little things, came to the hand, and flowers like jewels opened and shut amid the green reeds that grew out of the sand with its rich dusting of gold. Afterwards they floated with the immortal white swans that gently made way for them, bending their beaks to the still water that mirrored their snowy reflections. Afterwards they could ride the silky softness of the clouds calling on the Sky Wind to blow them to heaven's brink or perhaps play with the cherubs who loved to fly through the great soaring trees of the forest on pretty little dragons, beautifully caparisoned. It was all marvellous fun! But sometimes Titus wished he had a *job* to do. He was bursting with love and miraculous energy so sometimes his aura flared like the sun.

They were almost at the bottom of the slope and into the crystal fountain when a voice like a golden trumpet echoed across the hillside and a great beam of pure white light approached them at enormous speed.

"Titus, Thomas, I haven't seen you all day. A meeting

at the Archives Building, if you please. Titus, Thomas, hello…hello…"

Mr. Bliss, Titus thought in surprise. Archangel in charge of recruitments for guardian angels.

Immediately Titus popped out his wings. Thomas followed suit, both soaring high in the air above the tops of the eternally blossoming trees.

"Ah, there you are, boys. A busy morning ahead," Mr. Bliss said as soon as he saw them. Mr. Bliss stayed in place with a whirring of great wings, while Titus and Thomas flitted around him, all of them hundreds of feet off the ground.

Titus's radiant blue eyes shone with excitement. Just maybe one day he would get to be a guardian angel. "What's the meeting about, Mr. Bliss?" he asked with an eager inflection.

Mr. Bliss lifted his hands, light streaming from his fingertips. "Surely you can guess, Titus? Guardian angels have to be elected. We have to help our earthly friends. Poor souls, what would they do without us?"

What indeed!

The Great Hall of the Archives Building spired to God's glory, its walls sculptured of sparkling crystal inlaid with silver and gold. Today it was filled with luminous beings wearing exquisite flowing robes, rose, saffron, azure, rich emerald and crimson and a wonderful violet, so that everywhere one looked there was rainbow upon rainbow of rippling colour. The higher one went through the nine angelic ranks the more the myriad colours gave way to an extreme white radiance like that of Mr. Bliss who now stood before them in a blinding flash of light and a great rushing whirl of majestic white wings. Wings they all had in common, from the cute double and triple wings of the adorable little cherubs to the six-foot splendour of the most awesome angels of all, the Cherubim and Seraphim, the highest-ranking heavenly beings who guarded the Divine Throne. These exulted angels, naturally, did not attend staff meetings.

Mr. Bliss lost no time getting things under way. Angels were encouraged to speak of their experiences; looking after their earthly charges, leading them to the realm of Heaven, a place of such joy and beauty no human mind could encompass it; or sending souls back through the long tunnel between near death and eternity to fulfil their destiny. Guardian angel roles were renewed, legions more appointed in the twinkling of an eye. A few angels spoke of exhaustion, a state rare among their ranks, although it *was* known. One angel in particular, Lucas, told the most wistful tale of all. For twenty-four years he had been the appointed guardian angel of one Chloe Cavanagh who was proving such a handful Lucas feared he had suffered a temporary burnout. In fact he was feeling a loss of power in his lower right wing.

"It's not as though Chloe isn't a fine compassionate young mortal with considerable spirituality, but she's becoming something of a danger to herself," he told his brilliant audience. "She has a tragic history you see." Lucas went on to tell them Chloe had lost a sibling, a brother, Timothy, when she was six and the child barely eighteen months, leaving the family desolate. Then some two years ago tragedy struck again like a lightning bolt. Chloe's parents were involved in a car crash that killed her father and put her mother into a coma from which she hadn't emerged for months on end. The mother, still locked in a waking dream state, was now in a nursing home being cared for while Chloe tried to balance her career as a journalist in the high-powered world of network TV with being there for her mother.

Mr. Bliss was faced with a decision. To counsel Lucas and allow him to continue? Or allow Lucas a long rest and appoint a replacement. There were many positive angels he could rely on to do the job. Angels who wouldn't collapse under the strain.

As Mr. Bliss looked around thoughtfully a glowing young face distracted him. Titus, of course, his garments radiating a flawless blue light. Angels' beautifully sculptured tranquil features were seen mostly through a luminous haze rather like a vapour, but for some reason Titus's sparkling face was almost flesh and blood. He glowed, with his burnished rose-gold curls, brilliant blue eyes and a tracery of gold freckles that danced across his nose. Curious to have freckles in this perfect realm where the sun spilled only *adoration* onto God and His heavenly kingdom. Mr. Bliss had the feeling there might be much to learn about young Titus's past. Was it possible he had had an earthly life?

Even as Mr. Bliss considered a dip into Archives, Titus spoke up. "Please, Mr. Bliss, can't you give us little guys a go?"

There it was again. Those unusual words. *Guys?* Of course Titus liked reading about life on earth. Didn't they all!

Mr. Bliss folded his long, beautiful fingers together, the expression on his wonderful classic face not without sympathy. "Hmm. Not possible, young Titus, I'm afraid. I'm not saying not *ever* but not just yet."

"It could be the answer," Lucas suddenly interjected in a very deep mellow voice like a gong, reminding Mr. Bliss Lucas must be many thousands of years old. "I do realise Titus has had no experience but he's so full of pep he just might be able to keep up with Chloe."

Mr. Bliss's singular eyes that were very dark but sparkled with light, began to sharpen and glow. "I rarely if ever send anyone so young, Lucas," he pointed out gently.

"*You* started young, Mr. Bliss," Titus piped up.

Another thing that struck Mr. Bliss as odd. How did Titus know? "So I did," Mr. Bliss admitted.

There were chuckles all 'round, tender smiles for Titus.

"What joy it must be to be a guardian angel!" Titus exclaimed, bright curls abob. His expression was one of radiant hope.

Mr. Bliss pondered. Titus was an extremely helpful and cooperative young angel, given to playful games perhaps but excellent at supervising the cherubs. The experience of taking charge of a mortal life might catapult him into real responsibility, earn him his three-quarter wings. Really Titus wasn't all that different from himself at the same state of transformation.

"All right, Titus," Mr. Bliss announced to a rippling wave of applause and a familiar swishing of wings. "The position of guardian angel to Miss Chloe Cavanagh is yours as of now."

Titus strove to control the great flame of excitement that sent far-distant memories raying through his mind.

While the cherubs played ball with the low-hanging silver stars, Titus embarked on his great flight to earth, accelerating through the vast sea of clouds with a rhythmic swishing of his wings, revelling in the freshness of the wind, the extraordinary smell of earth's atmosphere as he entered it. While he watched the play of glittering golden sunlight on the near side of the planet, he was conscious of being happier than he had ever been in his experience. Maybe he had overdone the surging speed of descent. Even Heaven didn't seem real.

"Hold on, Chloe," he called in a sweet ecstasy, his glowing blue garments suddenly reflecting a white light. "I'm your guardian angel now. You can call upon my power."

To keep Chloe safe would be his great mission.

A great wave of love engulfed him. Not so much glory, but something of a different lustre; warm, human affection.

The soul remembers.

CHAPTER ONE

IT WAS well after nine-thirty when Chloe finally made it back to BTQ8, thinking she mightn't have a job at the end of the day. In the year since he had become Managing Director of the Brisbane link in the national network, McGuire had been reducing numbers at the drop of a hat. Downsizing, he said, in the quest to achieve better results. Not being a fan of McGuire's, Chloe chose to ignore the fact the TV station had been staging a remarkable comeback from near disaster under her old mentor, Clive Connor, who had since been moved on with a very generous redundancy package. She had never taken to McGuire, Clive's successor, but the Big Guys loved him. He was the Golden Boy with a big future in the industry. The man who could do no wrong. This might very well be her day to get the shove. The third monthly meeting she had missed in a row when she always started out with the very best intentions.

Hunching her shoulders against the heavy tropical downpour, Chloe dashed across the station car park and into the main building, struggling with her brolly which, being cheap, was playing up. When she looked up, McGuire was coming towards her. Six foot three of raw animal power. He had shoulders like a front rower which he had been apparently at University. She wouldn't have cared to be his opposite number. She didn't like men who were so dark, either. So in-the-face uncompromisingly male. For a man of Irish ancestry he was almost swarthy with thick jet-black hair he wore short to discourage the curl, a bronze skin and, it had to be admitted, rather fine near-black eyes with eyelashes most women would die for.

Chloe raised her hand and before she could help herself gave him a cheeky wave. Where for the love of mike was her sense of survival? Gone with the great wind from Hell that had blown away her entire world.

"Cavanagh, you're late," McGuire said with a touch of gravel, amused and irritated by the sort of cockiness she usually exhibited with him. He moved to join her, watching her fiddle with a floral umbrella that looked more like a child's sunshade, then flip back her trademark mane of red hair. It was pouring outside and her hair curled extravagantly in the humid heat. Corkscrew locks spilled forward onto her forehead and flushed cheeks. She looked ravishing, like a heavenly illumination in a Medieval manuscript where the artist used precious pigments and gold inks. All that was missing was the bright halo and she sure didn't deserve that. Three missed meetings in as many months. It made him so damned mad. Exaggeration. Exasperated. For some reason that evaded him, he had a soft spot for Cavanagh. Maybe it was the look of her, the finely constructed frame he would like to give a good shake. She appeared so light, so fragile, so feminine, the tender curves of her breasts, the willowy waist and delicate hips, the ballerina legs. Yet there was something strong about her, something supple and resilient that shone through the lightness. Of course he knew her tragic background, and that smote him. Not that she would ever confide in him. He was well aware of her hidden antipathy. Almost a revulsion, he sometimes thought, like a princess under siege with the barbarian at the gate. She had been ready to dislike him before he had ever been given the chance to open his mouth. He had no hand at all in Connor's sacking. Poor old Clive had brought it all on himself.

Chloe looking up at McGuire towering above her suddenly coughed, making him aware he had been staring. "In my office in ten minutes," he clipped off.

"Right, Chief." She just barely refrained from saluting him. What had stopped her? Perhaps because McGuire had swung back on her. Lord, for a big man he was remarkably light on his feet. A sudden vision of him in a tutu almost made her laugh aloud. "I'm so sorry I missed the meeting," she found herself saying hastily, "I do most humbly apologise."

It was so sweet he damn near lifted a hand to toy with her rain-sequined hair. Instead he asked sarcastically, "Another hot story breaking?"

"Could be a real scoop." It was a fib. She had made an unscheduled early morning visit to see her mother then got caught up in road works. No use to tell McGuire that. She could see the flint in his all-encompassing dark eyes.

"Sure you're not getting overly ambitious?" he challenged her, worried it might be the case. She had taken so many risks of late, even if they had managed to come off.

"It was you who persuaded us to lift our game, Chief," she pointed out innocently.

"Then I'll have to dissuade you from placing yourself in danger, as well. Get rid of these wet things then we'll have a nice chat."

Chat? Ha! As if she needed a chat with McGuire. Communications between the two of them were becoming increasingly edgy. She didn't know why she disliked him so much. Every other woman in the building fell in a swoon as he passed. Hers was a feline reaction, much like her marmalade cat confronted by a very large Doberman. Chloe raced on, greeting fellow workers to her left and right in her bright, friendly fashion, beaming at Mike Cole, senior sports writer, as he held the door of the outer office for her.

"Chloe, damned if I've ever seen anyone look so pretty in the rain," Mike exclaimed. "You've got messages, kid. They're on your desk. Better warn ya, Gabe was browned off when you didn't show up for the meeting."

Chloe looked up at Mike with a little grimace. "Don't I know. I saw the dear boy in the lobby. I started out so early, too, but I got caught up a traffic jam. Road works at Lang Park. Hopeless. They do everything right before an election. Fact is I called in on Mum. I had the weirdest dream last night. Mum was trying to tell me someone was coming. Pathetic isn't it?"

Mike shook his head in sympathy. He had been on his way out but decided to walk back with her. He and his wife, Teri, were very fond of Chloe. A frequent visitor to their home, she was the godmother to their newest baby, Samantha. Chloe had been given a very rough deal in life. But she was such a fighter. "What about a coffee?" he suggested.

"Love one. A rushed one," Chloe said. "I didn't have time for breakfast. McGuire gave me a drop-dead invitation. In his office in ten minutes." She glanced at her watch. "Correction, eight. He was looking at me so queerly as if he couldn't figure me out."

Mike snorted. "For such a tough guy, he's mighty easy on you." He walked to the coffee machine, came back with two steaming cups of black coffee. "And how is Mum?" he asked. He and Teri had accompanied Chloe to her mother's nursing home on several occasions. Delia Cavanagh was still a beautiful woman but the life switch had been turned off. Probably for good, Mike thought sadly.

"She looks so serene, Mike," Chloe said, a bright glitter of helpless tears in her dark blue eyes. "For all that has happened to her she doesn't seem to have aged a minute. It's like she's locked in time."

Mike shook his sandy head, receding rapidly at the hairline to his distress. "It's been hard on you, Chloe, but you're a daughter in a million." Chloe visited her mother on almost a daily basis when Mike knew her packed schedule. No wonder she looked like a breeze could blow her out of town.

Chloe gulped her coffee, too hot. "Why did it have to happen, Mike? Isn't it enough to lose your husband and child? I try, but I don't know that I believe in God anymore."

"Well, he sure isn't selling this world," Mike observed with a wry expression. "Maybe it's the next we should be aimin' for, kid."

"I think McGuire is of the opinion I'm trying to get myself killed."

Mike took a while to answer. "It makes sense, Chloe. Goodness knows Teri and I think you're the bravest girl in the world but you haven't quite come to terms with all the blows fate has dealt you. That's what worries Gabe."

Blue fire flashed from Chloe's beautiful eyes. "What would McGuire know about it? He knows nothing about me."

"Of course he does, Chloe. Don't take it so hard." Mike leaned back against Chloe's desk, a gangling attractive figure. "Your father was a well-known physician. It was in all the papers. Gabe has access to anything he wants to know."

"I wouldn't put a great deal of faith in McGuire's kind heart." Chloe started to push her coffee away. "I don't want him to know anything about me. I certainly don't want his pity."

"Chloe, love, settle down." Mike's voice carried a fatherly note. "I know you can't see this, but Gabe's a great guy."

"Who gave our good friend, Clive, the push and laid off Ralph and Lindsey," Chloe retorted.

"Connor had it coming. Be fair, in fact they all did. You have to admit Clive had lost his drive. I know we all liked him. You saw him as some sort of a father figure, but he totally lacked Gabe's skills, let alone brilliance."

"Gabriel McGuire, the one-man razor gang?" Chloe mocked, twiddling her fingers at a junior staffer.

"Everyone is cost conscious these days, Chloe. The shareholders want an adequate return and Gabe has to satisfy our national bosses. He's single-handedly pulled us from disastrous near-bottom ratings to giving Channel Nine a run for their money."

"All right, all right," Chloe sighed, wishing she had a croissant. She was hungry. "He's a dynamo but there's something kind of ruthless about him. I don't like men who look like that. So dark and overpowering."

"You just cut your teeth on poor old Clive," Mike pointed out gently.

"At least he was a gentle man."

"You just don't like Gabe, full stop."

"I told you. Something about him frightens me away."

"Hey, Chloe, like a muffin?" someone called. "Nice and fresh."

Chloe looked up as a young production assistant sauntered up to her, holding out a white paper bag.

"Gee, thanks, Rosie. I'm hungry, missed breakfast."

"Just popped into my head." Rosie smiled and moved off.

Chloe made short work of the delicious apricot muffin, wiped her mouth and fingers, then adjusted the collar of her yellow silk crepe blouse and stood up. "That's it, then. I'd better see McGuire."

"I'll walk out with you," Mike said. "I should have

been over at the Broncos training session ten minutes
ago.''

McGuire was watching her approach through the glass
wall of his office, motioning her in with a near pugilistic
lift of his arm. Needless to say he was on the phone, one
hand riffling through some papers, the other holding the
receiver slotted between his aggressive cleft chin and his
broad shoulder. Chloe took a seat, sitting upright, slender
legs neatly locked at knee and ankle. She wished now
she hadn't worn the yellow outfit, a favourite because it
brightened her mood, but the short skirt was undeniably
short. McGuire must have thought so, too, because his
eyes moved slowly over her legs before settling on her
face.

Drat. Why did he have to do that? He was carrying
on a high-powered conversation while his near-black
eyes almost bound her to the chair. He was openly studying her. Not politely, formally, but with confrontational
male interest. Chloe couldn't help knowing she was
pretty—other people said beautiful—but Chloe, at
twenty-four, was still a virgin with a very fastidious
mentality. Having sex, for Chloe, involved falling in
love, and Chloe knew better than anyone that love and
the loss of it meant terrible suffering. She had friends,
of course. Lots of friends. Male and female. But she
couldn't play the jump-into-bed game. One of the things
about McGuire that bothered her was his sexual cha-
risma, the certain knowledge that he would be a passionate maybe too demanding lover. She had known the
second she had laid eyes on him, felt his eyes on her;
recognised the looming battle ahead. She had readied
herself, immediately raising her defences against such a
threatening aura.

Now inexplicably she knew a bleak moment. She was
a mess. Had been since the fabric of her life had been

ripped apart. No man could ever put his heart in her hands. She wouldn't know what to do with it.

McGuire slammed the phone down and leaned across his massive mahogany desk, causing Chloe to audibly exhale.

"Tell me why you couldn't make the meeting?" he asked, almost gently for him.

For an instant, to her amazement, she considered telling him about her visit to her mother. What was the matter with her? "I was held up in traffic, Chief. They've decided at long last to do something about Lang Street."

His sensual mouth so clear cut, compressed. "Our meeting was set for 8:30 sharp. Road works commenced at 9:00 a.m. I heard it on early morning radio."

He would. "I'm sorry. I apologise." Even to her own ears she sounded sincere. "I know it's my job to attend. I fully intended to but I couldn't make it through the traffic." Heck, usually she threw down the gauntlet.

"Why can't you talk to me, Chloe?" He leaned back in the leather armchair, powerful body languid, two seeing eyes trained on her.

She got some kind of a mad rush just hearing him speak her Christian name. She flushed. "There's nothing to talk about, Chief. Outside work."

"We'll settle for that. You have a lot of potential, Cavanagh." He could see she was more comfortable with the surname, the odd, sweet, prickly little creature. "How long is it now since you joined BTQ8?"

"Of course you know. Four years. I came straight from University to cadet reporter. Clive taught me everything I know."

"I know he took you under his wing." Why not? She must have looked like a cherub. "Clive in his heyday as anchorman never had your flair. People are starting to get riveted to your on-camera reporting. That was a good piece you did on the Fairfield tragedy. I got a phone call from upstairs. Sir Llew was very pleased with the way you handled it.''

"Maybe, but I hate covering tragedies,'' Chloe said.

"We all do but it's our job. The public appetite for news is voracious. What sets you apart from many others is your compassion.''

Chloe looked down at the hands locked in her lap. "I didn't feel too compassionate staging a wait outside his house. I felt more like a vulture.''

"That's understandable but we all know about real life. A prominent politician about to be investigated for corruption. Not even his widow guessed he was going to commit suicide. I marvel she could talk at all.''

"Only to me,'' Chloe said, shaking her head sadly. "Only to Chloe Cavanagh. I don't know why.''

"I do,'' he said briefly. "You have a special knack for communicating with grieving souls.''

Why not? Chloe thought. I have a troubled soul myself.

"The only problem is, you're putting yourself too much in the front line.'' His voice switched suddenly, rasped.

"But this is a tough industry, Chief. No need to tell you that. I'm after the best story for the channel.''

He continued to appraise her as though seeking to see through to her soul. "You're not taking enough care and you know it. I know for a fact Rob has concerns.''

She was utterly taken aback. "Did he speak to you?''

"Most people outside of you, do.'' He smiled, a little tightly. "He's entitled. He's your sidekick, your photographer. He's very protective of you, like your mate Mike. But that was a very expensive camera that got wrecked. It's not your job to beard international con men in their den. You can leave that to our top investigative reporter.''

"But he didn't get the story, did he?" She spoke with a light note of triumph.

"No, but he has a black belt."

"Are you suggesting I learn karate?" she asked sweetly.

He shrugged a broad shoulder. "I'm suggesting you learn a few moves if you're going to continue to get yourself into situations where angels might fear to tread." His tone, tough and uncompromising, suddenly changed. "What would you think about taking over as anchorwoman at the weekend?" Hell, what a good idea. It just popped into his mind.

Chloe, too, was startled and looked it. She didn't want to take anyone's job but the thought excited her. "I don't know that I'm ready for anything like that," she evaded. The weekends gave her extra time with her mother.

"That doesn't sound like you, Cavanagh. Too boring?"

"I suppose you could say that," she sighed. "My talent is for getting a story, getting to the bottom of things. I'm not a talking head."

"You will be if I think you fit the bill." He had to think this thing through.

She sat very still. "You're the boss."

"And that continues to enrage you." There was a slight bunching of the muscles around his hard jawbone.

"Not at all." Her answer was surprisingly, disarmingly soft.

"So why look at me as if I'm a woman-eating tiger?"

Because you are and you'd better believe it. "You did send Marlene Attwell on her way," she pointed out.

"You admired her, did you?" His expression was cynical.

"Not quite. She was too bitchy for any of us to like her, but she's a professional. She looked good in front of the cameras and she has credibility."

He quelled a little rush of anger. Like some other people, he wasn't a forgiving soul. "She insulted a lot of powerful people once too often, Cavanagh. Not to set the story straight but to establish her own questionable style. Then as you say, her in-house standing was far from good."

Chloe nodded, looking suitably chastened. "I knew I wasn't going to leave your office with a big smile."

"Why so sure?" His black eyes sparkled with sardonic humour. "Mel Gibson will be in town the beginning of next month," he found himself saying. "A quick trip home to promote his new movie. He's willing to talk to us. I've had it confirmed."

Chloe looked back at him in astonishment. "You're surely not handing the job to me?" Her melodious voice, one of her big assets, took on a decided lilt.

"Can't handle it?" One black eyebrow shot up, giving him a rakish look. Surely he should be handing the interview to Jennifer?

"I'll have you know I once sat a few seats behind Mel on a plane." She smiled.

"Is that so? Then you won't want to miss this golden opportunity, either. He's happy to talk. Keep it short and keep it light."

"A pleasure." She totally forgot herself and beamed at him. Gosh, what was in that muffin? "It should be fun. They say he's the easiest person in the world to talk to. None of that Big Star ego. A down-to-earth Aussie. Won't Jennifer have her nose put out of joint?"

He held up a large palm. "There's no law against passing over our senior female reporter. Though Jennifer is never late, never misses meetings, and never gets herself involved in ongoing brawls."

"She'll certainly have something to say to me." Chloe smiled wryly. There were big jealousies abroad. Grudges. Undercurrents.

"That's your problem, Cavanagh." He stared at her for a minute or two. "I had intended to bawl you out, but I seem to have surrendered to your charm. You can go now. I'm busy. By the way, Sir Llew is giving a small party, which means roughly a hundred people, Saturday night. You'd better go out and buy yourself a new dress."

Anyone else but McGuire, she would have rushed to kiss his cheek. "You mean, I'm invited? That's a first."

His eyes sparkled sardonically. "Cavanagh, you're well on your way to becoming a high flier. I'm in a position to provide you with wings. Sir Llew wants four of us for company. Bright, engaging people, he said."

Chloe suppressed a snort. *Sure!* McGuire was brilliant. Engaging? *Never.*

He had to be a mind-reader because his dark eyes flashed. "Cavanagh, your face is so transparent you ought to wear a mask. The party's for Christopher Freeman, by the way." He named an international businessman of legendary wealth. Australian born, but currently residing in the U.S.A.

"The wild one." Chloe feigned a gasp. "Freeman has quite a reputation as a womaniser."

"Don't worry, I'll be there to protect you."

"No problem," Chloe responded blithely. "The likes of Christopher Freeman would get nowhere with me." A professional virgin with ice cubes rattling in her veins.

"I like that, Cavanagh," he said. "By the way, I'd like you to know our present weekend anchorwoman is looking to retire."

Chloe, walking to the door, turned back in surprise. "She never said so."

"She hasn't seen much of you of late," McGuire pointed out dryly, bewitched despite himself at the image of her. "For a girl who doesn't run with the crowd, you keep yourself mighty busy."

"I have a wonderful garden," she quipped.

"I admit you're a bit of a puzzlement, Cavanagh." He seemed to lose interest in her, reaching for a pile of papers. "Get Farrell in here, would you. I wish he had a few of your daredevil qualities." He glanced up casually. "I can give you a lift Saturday night if it would help. Drop you off home afterwards. The party's at Sir Llew's so it's going to be difficult getting parking near the house."

It sounded so simple yet it took her by storm, McGuire at close quarters? How claustrophobic could one get? Her moods were shifting madly back and forth. She couldn't account for it. "Thanks for the offer, Chief, but I'll be okay. I know my way around that neck of the woods."

"Well, the offer's open in case you change your mind. Oh, there's something else, too. I want a piece on Jake Wylie, the writer. I don't suppose you've gotten around to reading his book, *One Man's Poison?*"

Chloe's expressive face brightened. "As a matter of fact I have. I bought the hardback to see what all the fuss was about. A mite strong, but a cracking good story, very funny in places."

McGuire nodded. "He has all the makings. Our new great white hope, though he could pare down a bit on the sex. We don't need a potted course in how and where to do it."

I might, Chloe thought. "When would you want the piece?"

"Couple of weeks." His eyes were already on some newspaper clipping on his desk. "I'll give you time. Talk to him first. If you think he might have some on-camera potential we can find a spot for you both."

Just when she thought miracles were for someone else! "That's great!" From such a shaky start she thought a soft billowy cloud was beneath her. She could almost have gone skydiving. Sans parachute.

"Well?" He glanced up. For all his black eyes could bore a hole through her, their expression was almost kindly. "Everything okay, Cavanagh?" he jeered. Why did she have to look so beautiful, so delicate, so refined? It pierced his heart. She was usually such an uppity little devil, as well, with a lot of aggravation. Hair like flame, and a spirit to match.

"Everything's fine, Chief." Chloe tried to move off but she seemed stuck to the spot. "I suppose about Saturday it doesn't make sense taking two cars?" She *didn't* say that. She *couldn't* have said it. She began to seriously wonder what had befallen her. Maybe she should rush out and see a psychiatrist. This was McGuire, remember? The Wolf Man. Rumour tied him to Sir Llew's nubile daughter, the very attractive, high-profile party-goer, Tara.

"No sense at all," McGuire casually agreed. "Let's say I pick you up around eight o'clock."

So that was that.

Chloe fled McGuire's office before she found herself agreeing to dropping off his dry cleaning.

She and Bob were watching a clip on a monitor, one of her assignments due to air, when Rosie, clipboard in hand, bustled into the studio. "Listen, there's a protest meeting going on out at Ashfield parklands. Caller rang in. Usual thing, the greenies versus a developer. Rowlands, big shot. He wants to put in a shopping centre. Some of the locals are all for it but it would mean clearing a section of bushland where the koalas hang out."

"But surely the shire council is falling over itself trying to protect the wildlife?" Chloe lifted a brow.

"Up to a point. Hell, is it us or the koalas? They're

all over the place. Shift the little devils. All they need is a good feed of gum leaves,'' Rose muttered.

"The right gum leaves, Rosie. And they are being killed on the roads despite all the signs.''

"Want the job or not? We could send Pamela.''

"Pamela can't give an accurate account of anything. No, we'll be there.'' Chloe lost no time switching off the monitor. "If people are prepared to talk instead of shouting at one another they might be able to come up with a solution.''

"I know Rowlands,'' Bob, fortyish, almost as short as Chloe, said casually. "He's not much good at listening.''

"I don't suppose he'll be there. It'll be one of his people.''

They arrived at the Ashfield parklands in twenty minutes flat, Chloe jumping out almost before the BTQ8 van streaked up onto the footpath.

"Oh-oh, trouble,'' Bob chortled. "I wasn't expecting anywhere near as many people.''

"The more, the merrier,'' Chloe said briskly. "Get a move on, Bob. Let the camera roll.''

"People do wacky things when a camera's on them, Chloe,'' Bob called. "Take care. I don't want any more broken equipment.''

"Look at that! BTQ8,'' someone cried as Chloe made short work of crossing the parkland. "Chloe Cavanagh. That's a blessing. We might get heard.''

By the time Bob arrived with his camera, Chloe was right in the thick of it. She'd be on the side of the koalas, of course, but you couldn't please everyone. A lot of people seemed to want the shopping centre to go ahead, when as far as Bob could see there was a perfectly good one back down the road.

Chloe, one of those journalists who could really get people talking, worked the crowd briskly, taking opinions left and right. Most were concerned citizens, a few troublemakers, a couple from the lunatic fringe, their heads swaddled in red bandannas, with matching red waistcoats.

"They won't be satisfied until there are no koalas left." A very tall woman glowered.

The Rowlands' representative, an attractive, middle-aged woman, stylishly dressed, smiled and took Chloe's hand. "Mary Stanton, Miss Cavanagh, a pleasure. I'd like you to know no company is more environmentally conscious than we are at Rowlands, as I'm trying to tell these people."

This was howled down while Bob, busy videoing at Chloe's side, suddenly aimed the camera at a tree. Chloe looked up expecting to see a koala so dopey on gum leaves it hadn't noticed it was broad daylight and there was a rally in progress, only to find a boy about nine or ten waving at her when he should have been at school.

"You'd better come down," Chloe called, swinging 'round in surprise as a voice spoke softly in her ear. No one. That was odd. Disconcerted, she began again. "Come on down from there." The child was straddling a fairly high branch. None too substantial. Hadn't anyone noticed?

"I'm all right." He gave her a wide toothy grin, and slid further along the branch.

"The koalas have absolutely nothing to fear from us," the woman from Rowlands was saying very earnestly. "We try to get along with everybody. Not all of these trees are grey gums. The wildlife people will be only too pleased to rescue the very small koala population."

"Who does that boy belong to?" Chloe asked, trying to puzzle out where the voice had come from. A soft melodic voice, young, infectious, with a kind of bubbling happiness. She really didn't like the boy up there even if she knew she was being overly protective. It all had something to do with losing her little brother. Boys were always climbing trees. They had a lot of talent for it. But just looking up was giving her vertigo.

"All I want to ask is this," a stout woman in baggy jeans and a T-shirt two sizes too small, cried over the top of the male protester beside her. "Do we really need another shopping centre? There's a good one about a mile down the road."

"We don't all have cars, love," an elderly lady decorated in beads piped up. "The way I heard it they're going to sell out to a chain store. I feel terrible about the koalas but a new shopping centre right here would be exciting. I could walk over every day. Meet people."

"And you, sir?" Chloe asked, confronting an elderly man with military medals festooning his jacket.

"Why doesn't Rowlands pack up and go back to where he belongs," he barked.

"We can't give in to the greenies," a young mother with fuzzy blond curls, babe in arms, was exclaiming. "We all want the shopping centre. Everyone except *those* guys." She gestured towards the red bandannas.

"You couldn't put it somewhere else?" Chloe asked Mary Stanton doubtfully.

"Not a chance. We've done our homework. We have community backing."

At that there was an outcry, people on the fringes rushing in to protest, some with the light of battle in their eyes.

It should have made Chloe uneasy but for some reason she was focused on the boy in the tree. What was the big deal? It wasn't all that high. Yet...

When the branch suddenly snapped it was no real surprise to Chloe. People underneath panicked, running out of harm's way, but Chloe, the slender, the fragile, the petite, zeroed in. She wordlessly put up her arms, waiting for the boy to topple into them.

Incredibly he did.

People gaped in amazement, blinking like rabbits, honestly not believing their eyes. Chloe was spinning across the springy grass almost dancing, holding the boy aloft before they both suddenly fell, full stretch, side by side, to peals of merriment.

The crowd, a moment before in full roar, fell silent, then broke into a delighted round of applause and some giggles, as first Chloe then the boy leapt lightly to their feet. "How the heck did she do that?" one of the red bandannas asked in wonderment.

"She must be pumping iron," his companion replied.

"Look, isn't that sweet?" the old lady cried.

The boy had leaned up to kiss Chloe's cheek, fumbling in his pocket for a piece of paper for her autograph. How could a skinny, five-three maybe five-four girl with a mop of wild red hair have the strength to catch him? He figured she had to have had some help from her guardian angel. His had disappeared the same day his dad had left home and never returned.

Everyone wanted to shake Chloe's hand.

"It was nothing," she felt compelled to say, still trying to grasp how the boy had seemed to weigh little more than Samantha, her baby goddaughter.

"Adrenaline," an elderly man, an ex-professor explained. "One becomes absolutely superhuman in a crisis. Wonderful, my dear, and your cameraman got it."

"What a turn-up that was!" a protester in scruffy running shoes cried.

The crowd was delighted, for the first time turning to one another, wondering, smiling, ready for a friendly chat.

"You know there's another possible site we passed on the way," Chloe addressed Mary Stanton, who was giving her wide-eyed attention. "Huge corner block near a nursery. A For Sale sign on it.'' Had she really noticed all that?

"Old Waverley's farm,'' Military Medals supplied. "He won't sell to any developer,'' he added sternly.

"You tried him, did you?'' Chloe prompted the still confused Mary.

"We certainly did, but he was very hostile,'' Mary managed ruefully.

"Try him again,'' Chloe suggested. "He's sitting in the blue Holden over there.'' She waved a hand.

Mary took a deep breath. "You know him, do you?'' As she had just witnessed, anything was possible.

"Never met him in my life, but I'm sure that's he.'' *My goodness, why?* Chloe thought. If she was psychic, she wanted to be the first to know.

"I can't bowl up to a stranger.'' Mary turned to Chloe, flustered. "You could be mistaken.''

"All right, anyone know Mr. Waverley?'' Chloe's voice echoed like a silver bell.

Sure enough, Running Shoes answered. "Old Jack? He's sitting over in his car. Probably hoping to bump up the price of his farm. That's where the shopping centre should be, if you ask me. We could all agree to that.''

"Well, I never!'' Mary Stanton thrust her shoulder bag under her arm. "Normally I don't revel in these contentious occasions but this has been really *amazing.* I just might be able to get Mr. Waverley to listen.'' She touched Chloe's arm. "Thank you, dear. I've never seen a young woman so vibrant with life. Or so *strong.*''

"Keep me posted,'' Chloe called, shooting a hand behind her to grasp a bony wrist. "Just a minute, Archie.''

The boy's mouth fell open in astonishment. This Chloe was a female to be reckoned with. "How did you know my name?'' He grinned.

"You told me, didn't you?'' Chloe looked down brightly.

"No, I didn't." Archie blew out his breath. She didn't look at all different from the people around her but she certainly had powers. "I'm called after me grandfather, Mum and I are going to live with him."

"You can tell me all about it when we give you a lift home," Chloe said, "but first things first, Archie. Why aren't you at school?"

"They won't miss me," Archie whispered. "The koalas are my friends. I don't want to see them go."

Around them the protest meeting was breaking up, the crowd faintly dazed, collectively beginning to lose all memory of that extraordinary incident. If old Waverley would sell out, things could work out. That Chloe Cavanagh was a magical girl.

"I can't understand it," Bob said as they stood watching the film run through the monitor. "I've got everything bar the moment when you caught the kid and started your astonishing dance."

"The crowd surging around didn't help, Bob. Sure you had the camera trained on me?"

"Are you crazy?" Bob gave her an injured glance. "Of course I'm sure. Hell, Chloe, you should be ashamed of yourself for asking. I'm one of the best in the business."

"Well, you're never going to live down this one, Bobby." Chloe patted him kindly on the shoulder. "All we have is this shot of Archie and me in deep conversation."

"It was a miracle," Bob suddenly announced. "I know it. How am I supposed to video a miracle? It just doesn't happen."

"If you say so, Bobby." Chloe laughed. "I've got to tell you, I've never felt like that in my entire life. It was like some other being got hold of Archie. I suppose it's not all that unusual. I had a friend who lifted a car off a neighbour's child. The mother backed out the garage not realising her little girl was there. Ian jumped the fence when the mother screamed and lifted the rear of the car right off the toddler. Do you know, she wasn't even hurt.''

"I'd say the kid had a darn good guardian angel." Bob scratched his head in some perplexity. "Let's run the tape through again. I want to check if something's wrong."

They were still talking about it in the corridor when McGuire happened along.

"Okay you two? You look like you're back from a space flight." He paused for a moment to study them.

"There are some things in life, Chief, that just don't add up," Bob said. "Chloe and I were at a protest meeting a couple of hours ago—"

"Cavanagh never outlives her enthusiasm for protests." McGuire's black eyes were mocking.

"Don't I know it. But she's so helpful. People love talking to her. Anyway, this most amazing thing happened."

"Tell me," McGuire urged, his deep voice a purr.

"It's nothing," Chloe murmured briefly, feeling embarrassed.

"Nuthin' don't say it." Bob tilted his head to address his tall Chief. "There was this kid up a tree. About ten, stopped home from school so he could join the protest. Course the mother didn't know. This big branch snapped under him. You had to hear the noise. Everyone scattered but not Chloe. While we all thought the kid could break a leg, Chloe, wait for it, positions herself like Arnie Schwarzenegger while the kid takes a nosedive."

"No. So what did he break?" McGuire asked laconically.

"What I'm trying to tell you, Chief, is Chloe *caught* him."

McGuire said nothing for a moment, not taking his eyes off Chloe's flushed face, then he patted Bob's arm. "Sounds like you two stopped off for lunch. Cracked a bottle of wine."

"Never on the job," Chloe said. "I'm still not sure how I did it. I've had this funny voice in my ear all day."

"A visit to your doctor might help. You wouldn't have it on camera, I suppose, Bob?" McGuire asked.

"Now this is the really *amazing* part. I got everything else but some outside force seemed to put the camera into freeze."

McGuire set his fine white teeth. "You'll have to excuse me, folks. Ordinarily, I love to hear the mad stories you two make up."

"It wasn't a story, truly. I did catch him," Chloe said.

McGuire wasn't convinced. "You? Listen, you look like you'd have trouble emptying your shopping trolley. Heck, what do you weigh?" He took a step towards her, eyeing her slight figure, then before Chloe could move he swept her off her feet in one lightning-fast movement. "I'd say about fifty-four kilos." He actually bounced her like a baby. "Am I right?"

She was utterly devastated. Her heart did a mad somersault and the blood whooshed in her ears. *"Put me down."*

"Soon." McGuire saw the rush of feeling flash through her eyes. Probably saw herself as Jessica Lange borne aloft by King Kong. "It's a joke, right?" he asked with elaborate casualness.

"There were plenty of witnesses." Bob was fascinated by the sight of Chloe looking like a porcelain doll in the Chief's arms. He had to be dreaming all of it. "I can find you someone to speak to," he offered.

McGuire laughed. "So there's magic in you, Cavanagh." Just holding her made him feel bedazzled.

"Magic to move people. Catch them if you have to. That has to be the reason. It's also quite possible you two screwballs dreamed the whole thing up."

Bob looked shocked. "We've got too much respect for you, Chief, to waste your time."

McGuire looked down at Chloe, noting every nuance of her expression. The scent of her was in his nostrils; honeysuckle, golden wattle, the fragrance of Spring.

"Chief," she said, exasperated. She knew he could hear her unsteady breathing. Those smouldering black eyes zooming in on the telltale rise and fall of her breast.

"This is where it all falls apart, Bob. Cavanagh couldn't possibly break the fall of a ten-year-old boy. You know it. I know it."

"What happened was a miracle," Bob proclaimed like a convert.

"Nope. You're just mad." McGuire lowered Chloe to her feet, keeping his hand on her shoulder for a moment as though recognising she was very fluttery. "Sorry, you two. Got to run. You might like to be there when the jury returns a verdict on the Chandler case. I've just had a tip-off it could be late this afternoon."

"Does this mean you still trust us?" Chloe challenged.

McGuire looked back over his shoulder, gave a twisted grin. "Sure, Cavanagh. What you obviously need is a good night's sleep."

"I guess you could call it mass hysteria," Bob said later.

Chloe looked away from him. She could still feel McGuire's strong muscular arms wrapping her body. She could still feel the shock waves, the chemistry as old as time, the brush of heat. It shamed her. "Let's put it out of our minds," she advised. We have to concentrate on the Chandler job. It has to be guilty."

"There's always a shock verdict, Chloe." Bob sighed.
"I've discovered that. Hang on a minute and I'll get
another tape. There must have been something wrong
with the other one."

CHAPTER TWO

BEFORE she left Friday, Chloe popped her head around the door of McGuire's office. He was on the phone and he gave her a quick warning look: Don't interrupt.

"Right, what is it?" he gritted when he finished what was clearly an aggravating call.

Unbelievable! Why had she accepted his offer to drive her to the party?

"I wasn't sure if you knew where I lived."

"Piece of cake, I've run past the house several times."

"Whatever for?"

He looked back at her, a tight smile at the corner of his mouth. "Why not? I like to know all I can about the staff. Bit big for you, isn't it?" It was a beautiful old Colonial, the family home, he had since been told, but it had to be a drain on her resources, physical and financial.

"I wouldn't want to be anywhere else," she said simply.

He was sympathetic to that. "So see you, then."

"Fine. Wonderful." She backed out quickly, muttering under her breath. Maybe he would be in a better mood tomorrow. If not she would simply call a cab.

Saturday morning found her shopping for the week's supplies. Nothing much. She lived on fresh fruit and salads. She bought ham and cheese from the delicatessen, a roast chicken, a couple of loaves of bread she could pop into the freezer. There was no time to cook.

35

Mostly she didn't have the inclination. Not after long hours on the job. Occasionally she and her friends went out to dinner when she made up for the slight deprivations. Early afternoon was spent in the garden trying to bring some semblance of order to the large grounds she was gradually turning to low-maintenance native plants. Her mother had adored her garden. So had her father when he had the time. Now they were both gone from this place.

A sense of loss beat down on Chloe but she tried to fight it back. In the early days after the double tragedy, she had experienced an overwhelming debilitating grief, a sense of futility and emptiness. How could she live without her father *and* mother? But when her mother had come out of the coma and into a waking dream state Chloe had started to fight back. She wanted to be around when her mother was returned to *full* life, even when the doctors told her day after day that was never going to happen.

Her skin glistening with tears, Chloe dug in a flowerbed overflowing with daisies, petunias, pink and white impatiens, double pelargoniums with a thick border of lobelia. A magnificent Iceberg rose climbed all over the brick wall that separated the house from their neighbour's, spilling its radiance all over the garden. Her mother loved white in the garden, the snow white of azaleas, candytuft, the masses and masses of windflowers she used to plant. The azaleas continued to bloom prolifically in Spring but she couldn't afford the time for all the rest. Eventually she supposed she would have to sell the house. McGuire was right. It was too big. Once they had been very comfortably placed. Not rich, but her father had been a well-established specialist physician. Now money was going out at a frightening rate. It worried her dreadfully she might have to shift her mother from her nursing home. "Jacaranda Hill" was one of

the very best, a large converted mansion with beautiful
grounds and a reputation for excellent care. Chloe
couldn't fault the way her mother was being looked after, but it was very expensive.

Mid-afternoon found her pushing her mother's wheelchair across the nursing home's lawn, finding a lovely
shady spot under one of the many magnificent blossoming jacarandas that gave the nursing home its name. A
man-made lake had been constructed some years back
in a low-lying area of the garden, now its undulating
edge was totally obscured by the lush planting of water
iris, lilies, ferns and ornamental aquatic grasses. A small
section of the large pool was taken up with beautiful
cream waterlilies but the important thing for the patients
was the sparkle and reflection of the water, the way the
breeze rippled over its surface, marking the green with
molten silver.

Chloe in jeans and a simple T-shirt sat on the grass
beside her mother's chair, holding lovingly to her
mother's quiet unresponsive hand. Strangely, despite all
evidence to the contrary, Chloe never had the feeling her
mother didn't recognise her, though the blue eyes so like
her own seemed to be looking into the next world already. Totally without fear, but inturned. Maybe she was
seeing visions, Chloe thought. Maybe she was in spirit
with her husband and son, or there could be dozens of
responses trapped inside her head. Chloe never saw her
intense dedication to her mother as a duty. Being there
was simply a measure of her love. As always on her
visits, Chloe told her mother what was happening in her
life. She spoke as though her mother was fully present
and as interested in what Chloe had to say as she had
been in the old days when life was full of sparkle and
neither had questioned the happiness and stability of
their family life. She spoke about her ongoing dealings
with McGuire, what she was doing around the house and

garden, her various assignments and, of course, the extraordinary incident of the day before. The really *odd* thing was, Chloe's own memory of it was beginning to blur. She had to really concentrate before it all faded.

"I don't believe I was holding him at all," she confided to her mother in remembered amazement. "I could feel the warmth of this solid little boy's body. I could see the sheen of perspiration on his skin. The crowd was speechless. There I was waltzing around with Archie quite calmly. It just doesn't make sense. It was like I was transformed. McGuire thought we were having him on. He told me to go home and get a good night's sleep. But it *did* happen. That's the mystery. What do you think?"

Then came the shock.

"What?" Chloe, who had been looking out toward the lake whilst she was speaking, shot a startled upward glance at her mother. Her warm voice had clearly sounded in Chloe's mind.

But Delia Cavanagh's expression was unchanged. A frisson of something that was almost awe rippled through Chloe's body from brain to heart to the tip of her toes. Was she going mad? In some way she couldn't possibly fathom, she was convinced her mother had spoken to her at some level. Some subtle communication.

"Mumma!" She clutched her mother's hand more tightly, finding what was happening difficult to grasp, but there was no response on her mother's tranquil face nor did a muscle move.

"Oh, God!" Chloe tried desperately to collect herself before she burst into tears. She wasn't entirely right in the head. That was it. Psychological damage from severe trauma was a reality of life. Yet she *had* caught that whisper as it rippled past her ear. She had. She had. What else did she have to cling to but hope? Her faith in God had lessened over this terrible time.

Chloe struggled to her feet, upset and without direction, only, she realised with a rush of sensation, someone was giving her a helping hand. On her feet she stopped abruptly as though she could very easily bump into them. She even rubbed her hands together waiting for the electric little tingle to subside.

"This is insane," she said out loud, causing a passing nurse to stare at her. Yet there was comfort, an easing of her grief.

Chloe dusted off her jeans and began to push her mother's wheelchair in the direction of the pretty little summerhouse at the far end of the lake. A beautiful pink rose clambered over the white lattice walls, and the pair of stone deer donated by a patient's grateful family, flanked the entrance. It was their usual route. What was unusual was her extraordinary notion this third person, this *invisible* person, accompanied them on their journey. The person who had taken her by the hand.

Spirit power, Chloe thought, giving her mother's shoulder a gentle squeeze. She was going to have to start saying her prayers again. Renew the communication she so abruptly had broken off with a great and loving God.

Chloe had never taken as much trouble over a party; never spent so much time trying on different dresses, or regarding herself so long and critically in the mirror. She was down to two dresses now. The lime green silk, long with a halter neck, or the floral-print chiffon, sleeveless with a ruffle around the crossover V-neck and a sort of handkerchief skirt. Each conveyed a certain look. Cool and classic, or that delicate ethereal look she couldn't seem to escape. Neither dress was new. She didn't feel she had the right to spend the money anymore, but they were still in fashion. Maybe the flowered chiffon had the edge. The very feminine look was in and the fabric was beautiful, rose pink peonies with a tracery of jade leaves

on a turquoise ground. The chiffon would have to do.
She could be the Spring fairy.

A very strange feeling ran through her all the time she
dressed. Pleasurable anticipation, normal enough in the
circumstances, but she was haunted by the element of
sexual awareness. Since when did she find McGuire
sexy? Since when was she all atremble at the thought of
being close to him? She disliked the man, was highly
wary of him and had said so at length. Nevertheless she
was excited and it sparkled in her looks.

Chloe opened the front door to McGuire as the grandfather clock in the living room was chiming eight. She'd
known it was to be a black tie occasion but she hadn't
expected to see him look so—gosh, she couldn't avoid
the word *splendid*, in evening dress. She almost had to
look away.

"Hi," he offered with dark, gleaming eyes. "You
look enchanting." A rare enough quality, but it was true.
Tonight she wore her marvellous hair—red, amber, gold,
a combination of all three—in an unfamiliar style. Pulled
back off her face and arranged in a thick upturning roll
but molten little tendrils sprang out around her face and
nape. Her deep blue eyes, large and liquid, had picked
up the colour of her dress, her skin was blushed porcelain, her mouth surprisingly full, tender, even a little
pouty. He wondered as he always did what it would be
like to kiss it, to open soft lips with the tip of his tongue.

She was always immaculately turned out in her little
blouses and skirts, the snappy little suits, but he had
never seen her in an evening dress before. The frothy
shimmering ruffle of the bodice plunged low to reveal
the shadowed cleft between her delicate breasts. He had
to fight down the irresistible urge to reach for her. He
knew she would only recoil in dismay.

"Why, thank you." She dropped a graceful little bob,
some note in his voice had got to her. This was McGuire,

remember? Her old combatant and sparring partner. "Would you like to come in for a moment?" Keeping him on the doorstep was impossibly rude.

"Yes, I would." He stepped across the threshold, looking like someone who could very easily mix it with the mega-rich. "This is a wonderful old house," he said almost wistfully, glancing down the wide hallway with its glowing parqueted floor and rosy Chinese rug. A circular rosewood library table holding a jade horse on a carved stand and a large crystal bowl massed with white roses stood midway between the graceful arches that led to the formal rooms.

"I love it." Chloe smiled, standing at his shoulder. "Let me show you through, that's if we have time."

"I'd like that." Amazingly his whole expression had softened. "The house was built by your great-grandfather, I understand." It had heritage listing he knew.

Chloe paused, lifting her chin. She so hated people talking about her. "Who told you that?"

He gave an easy shrug of his powerful shoulders, breaking the slight tension. "I do a lot of checking."

"I suppose it goes with the territory," she answered wryly.

"You should know, Chloe."

At the use of her Christian name, so honeyed and intimate, a mild giddiness overtook her.

"If one could really chart the course of one's life, this is just the sort of house I'd have liked to live in," he said.

"Really? I thought you'd like something very modern, very strong, with sweeping clear places." And terrible pictures that looked like cubic puzzles on the walls.

Once again his black eyes roved over her, checking out her too innocent expression. "I won't say I don't like to integrate old and new, but in terms of architecture

I love these old Queensland Colonials with their sweeping verandah and white iron lace. They're perfect for the subtropical climate. I particularly like the high ceilings and large rooms.''

"A big man would." She was surprised by how sweetly that came out. They walked side by side, Chloe in her exquisite flowered chiffon, McGuire in his beautifully cut evening clothes. It was all so extraordinarily civilised.

"Someone had a very graceful hand with the decorating," he commented.

Chloe felt her throat tighten. "My mother." She couldn't say a word more.

He admired the classic elegance of the living room, the mix of fine antique pieces with overstuffed chintz-covered sofas and armchairs in shades of ivory, peach and rose. A huge gilt-framed antique mirror hung over the fireplace with its beautiful white marble surround, and he walked towards it, studying the detail. "It must comfort you to have the stamp of her personality all around you."

"Sometimes," Chloe said softly, surprised by his perceptiveness. "Other times it hurts dreadfully." She gestured towards an adjoining room. "Come through to the library. It's my favourite room."

The instant before she turned on the lights, Chloe came close to believing someone was sitting in her father's wing-back chair beside the fireplace. She even drew in her breath.

"Everything okay?" McGuire stood very close, tall, powerful, protective.

"Of course." It had to be an optical illusion. Particularly when she had the sense of someone *small.* Her father had been almost as tall as McGuire, but a completely different build, very spare with long, elegant limbs. She didn't feel ready to deal with the odd things that were happening to her. She couldn't dismiss them, either.

"You've gone a little pale."

"I'm fine," she said huskily.

"Do you ever feel nervous by yourself?"

"I've got my guardian angel on call." Her eyes mirrored the sudden comfort that wrapped her soul.

"I'm glad." His finger touched the tip of her nose, gentle as a feather, then he turned to inspect the large, graceful room.

He looked around keenly, showing considerable interest in everything, Chloe thought, the plaster work, the cedar panelling, the inbuilt floor-to-ceiling bookcase, the leatherbound gold-foiled volumes. Even the 19th-century French gilt chandelier. If she gave him enough time he might make an offer for house and contents. "You must have enjoyed growing up here," he murmured, the slight moodiness of his expression lending him the disturbing charm of Jane Eyre's Rochester.

She couldn't speak for a moment until her voice was under control. Though he was far from *her* ideal, he was, she began to realise, a ruggedly handsome man who carried himself superbly. "Where *did* you grow up?" she asked gently. The graciousness of her own surroundings were definitely having their effect on her, but he smiled his familiar taut smile.

"A small town outside Sydney, but I guess what you'd call the wrong side of the tracks."

For once a sharp retort was easy to resist. "But you've come a long way."

"That was the intention, Chloe. As far away as I could get." The intonation was harsh. He shot back a cuff and glanced down at his gold watch. "Thank you for showing me your beautiful home. I'd like to see more, but I think we should be on our way."

"Of course." She flushed a little and as he passed

her, he very gently stroked her cheek. "Now I know why you're such a princess," he said in a deep, low voice.

They were gliding away from the house before she could contribute another word. "I didn't know you drove a Jaguar?" It was, in fact, a late model.

"I've been promising myself one since I was a kid."

"It's my kind of car." She smiled.

"Of course. You didn't think I was going to pick you up in what I drive to work?"

"I didn't think at all."

"Why's that, Cavanagh?" He shot her a challenging glance.

"Hey, you've been calling me Chloe," she protested for a second, strangely hurt.

"And you've been calling me nothing at all. To my face. I know what you call me behind my back."

"Oh, please, don't believe it all." Chloe was embarrassed. "We're going to a party, remember?" She realised with a sense of shock she wanted to maintain the unusual harmony that flowed between them.

"So, *say* it, then," he prompted gruffly.

"Say what?" Inside the soft enfolding darkness of the beautiful car with its smell of fine leather mingled with her own perfume, the atmosphere was oddly intimate.

"My name," he answered, shooting a glance at her. "Gabe, Gabriel, whatever you like."

Chloe sucked in her breath. "Gabriel, the Messenger of God. You must admit it's a shade incongruous with your powerful physique and dark colouring."

"You'd relate better to Lucifer?"

She could see his eyes, dark and shimmery like the night. "Even for you that's too scary. What do you say to a truce? I'll call you Gabriel for the night, if you continue to call me Chloe. We can revert to our normal selves Monday morning."

"Suits me." He nodded. "I mean, can you imagine us being friends?" He sounded openly mocking and he had good reason.

"You know what they say, anything's possible," Chloe replied jauntily.

"I don't think you could handle it, Cavanagh." He glanced at her briefly. God, she was exquisite.

"You gather correctly."

"I'm just your normal guy."

She laughed, a sound of pure rejection. "No, you're *not.*"

"I'd still like to get this whole thing cleared up. What *exactly* about me bothers you so much?"

Everything. Your looks, your force of character. "Gabriel I have no problem with you at all," she said sweetly.

"Oh, but you *do.* Don't smile about it."

"Well..." She considered. "You really like to stir me up."

He made a deprecating sound. "I have to admit I do."

"And you have your own reasons for it."

"True. But I seek to help you, Chloe, before you run yourself ragged. I might be a bit abrasive at times but I believe my intentions are good. You did what you liked under your old boss."

Chloe admitted that inwardly. "Clive went a lot earlier than he should have."

His smile was faintly crooked. "You're just prejudiced. We're on the same side, you know, even if our relationship hasn't been all that smooth."

"Clive didn't bark at me." She smiled.

"And what do you think the answer to that may be? You can't twist me around your little finger, neither can you march in and out of my office uninvited."

The colour in Chloe's cheeks deepened. "That's not true. I always knock."

"When you remember to. Anyway that's all camouflage. I think the problem is *physical*."

She was glad of the darkness to cover her shock. This was unchartered country. "Well, you do have a lot of *presence*," she managed. In fact it was particularly powerful.

"Really? You make me feel like Conan the Barbarian." His glance mocked them both. "All those haughty little high-born expressions."

"I can't see what *I* think should bother you at all."

"Hey! I'm asking the questions," he drawled.

"All right. Fire away. I'll have to rack my brains for a soothing answer. If it's any comfort to you, I know at least a dozen women in the building who find you extremely attractive."

"Fourteen at the last count," he said laconically.

"What I can't figure out is why you're not married." She *didn't* say that, did she? Someone had cast a spell on her.

He shot her a sardonic glance. "If I asked *you*, would you accept?"

For a split second her heart quaked in her breast. She was no match for McGuire. "You've got to be joking!"

"No," he said in a practical voice. "You have a lot going for you. You're beautiful, you're brainy, a bit on the volatile side but certainly not dull. You know the industry, so you wouldn't be wondering all the time where I was."

Chloe shook her head, glancing at him in slight alarm. "Not a good idea at all. You and I as marriage partners doesn't fit my wildest scenario."

"Okay, Chloe. I'm just having fun. You don't trust *anyone* with your heart?" The question was so smooth and gentle she was taken aback.

She answered sadly as if to herself. "No."

One wouldn't have to look too closely at the reasons.

At the pain and despair which had to be in her heart. "I believe in love, Chloe," he said with great dignity. "I've no good reason to, but I do. I had a very bleak childhood." He could have said terrifying with a violent father and a mother trapped by fear. "All I could ever think was, run, run, run, but I stayed for my mother's sake."

Chloe was stunned by the revelation. "Gabriel, I'm so sorry." A tremendous sympathy flowered from her body.

"Gracious lady." His voice sounded both tender and a little scathing. He glanced at her. How beautiful...how beautiful. He had craved beauty all his life, yet something about her made his heart throb painfully. It had from that very first day when she walked into his office and he could only stare. "No need to be, Chloe." He spoke dismissively. "It might have been a struggle but it made me tough." His rugged face was dark and shadowed. "I know the toughness bothers you."

Chloe couldn't answer. There was no way to deny it, but tender-hearted, she sensed she had wounded him. This vigorous, confident man who held his head so proudly. She would never have suspected it.

A hush fell over the interior of the car. It was far from relaxed; strong emotion had touched them and a force was at work.

Sir Llew Williams, owner and chairman of BTQ8 along with other profitable enterprises, lived in a very large Mediterranean-style villa on what was commonly known as Riverside, Millionaire's Row. Cars lined both sides of the wide street which at the height of summer became a brilliant avenue of scarlet as the giant poincianas burst into hectic flower. McGuire didn't even attempt to find a parking spot but drove straight up to the tall, decorative wrought-iron gates, where he was admitted by a security guard who checked his name against a list.

"Who's a favourite, then?" Chloe gently crowed.

"Don't knock it." He spoke dryly. "You wouldn't have been able to do much walking in those shoes." He glanced down at her narrow high-arched feet crisscrossed with a few flimsy turquoise straps.

"Listen, you know you don't have to bother about me," she said as he came around to the passenger side to help her out.

"Chloe, I'd be glad to."

Once out of the Jaguar she let go of his hand quickly. She was getting these intense tingles all the time. "That's very kind of you, Gabriel, but I don't want you to think you must look out for me. I'm used to fending for myself."

He hunched his powerful shoulders slightly. "Sure, but I'm here if you need me."

She gave him a faintly puzzled little smile. "Why the concern, sweet though it is?"

"It won't take Freeman long to notice you," he said bluntly, taking her arm and leading her along the flood-lighted garden path.

"Goodness, a man who's had *three* wives already." Chloe sounded shocked.

"It's fairly obvious he's looking for number four."

"I daresay that's possible, but you have nothing to fear. All those tabloid stories! He's a dreadful man in some respects."

He smiled grimly. "Chloe, it might be an idea if you kept your voice down. It has the peal of a silver bell."

"Sorry." The warning wasn't lost on her. "None of us is perfect."

"That has to be right, but some are worse than others. I'm just begging you to be very, very careful. Two of his wives had flaming red hair."

Chloe laughed quietly. "Keeping it flaming must have cost a good deal of money. I appreciate your concern, Gabriel, but really, I can take care of myself."

"Just don't listen to his pitch." As they neared the door, his words were just barely audible. "I feel sure he's going to make it."

Which was exactly what happened.

The instant they moved into the marble foyer, Tara Williams detached herself from a laughing group, charging towards McGuire. She grasped his hand and reached up on tiptoe to kiss his cheek.

"Gabe, you gorgeous man! How wonderful to see you. Daddy said to take you to him the moment you arrive. And..." She paused, looking wide-eyed and guileless. "Chloe, isn't it?"

Of course she knew. Chloe was a familiar sight on television. "Chloe Cavanagh, Miss Williams." Chloe smiled. "I'm so pleased to be invited to your lovely party."

"Daddy likes to have a few of the staff in from time to time," Tara answered ungraciously, though she attempted to conceal it with a smile. Cushioned by so much wealth she obviously felt she could say and do as she pleased, Chloe thought. She watched as Tara looped two hands around McGuire's arm, staring mesmerically into his face with eyes that were a startling ice blue. Her rich brown hair fell thick and straight just clear of her shoulders; her dress was very glamorous, long, slinky, red silk-jersey, with a rather daring keyhole cutout. In Chloe's opinion she was showing too much bosom, but it seemed to be the fashion and no doubt the men didn't mind.

Chloe went on smiling prettily even when it was evident Tara was about to carry McGuire off, leaving Chloe to her own devices. It might have been particularly appalling had she been shy, but Chloe was no shrinking violet. "Excuse us, won't you?" Tara tossed Chloe another of her big courtesy smiles. "I'll send a friend of mine over. Pru Gregory. You'll like her. We went to school together. I simply must hear what Gabe's been up to."

McGuire in fact was regarding Tara rather sardonically. Which was odd. Surely with all the rumours they got on better than that? It even appeared to Chloe he was about to ask her to join them and thus spoil Tara's evening, when Sir Llew strode towards them. Tall, heavily built, with the ice cube eyes he had passed on to his daughter, he had a mane of silver hair so thick it looked like it had been professionally blow-dried, which for all Chloe knew it could have been, and jet-black bushy eyebrows, which some thought dashing and others ridiculous. There was no Lady Williams. Tara's mother had literally given up the ghost when Tara was an incredibly spoiled fourteen and the number one person in her father's life. Which probably explained why Sir Llew had thought it best never to remarry.

"Gabe, my dear fellow." Sir Llew put out his hand as if he had never felt more fond of anyone in his life. "I'm so glad you've arrived. I want you to meet Christopher."

McGuire looked amused. "I did meet him once in Washington when I did a stint there, Sir Llew. He would have forgotten."

"Actually, no," Sir Llew chortled roguishly. "You weren't exactly writing nice things about him at the time. Ah, Chloe." He turned to include Chloe in his expansive smile. "How lovely you look, my dear. You must come, as well. Chris adores a pretty face."

"You're a hell of a lot more than a pretty face," McGuire muttered beneath his breath to Chloe as Sir Llew led them all full steam across the glittering foyer to one of the most over-decorated living rooms Chloe had ever seen. Though she was far from being a minimalist, she thought the room could do with a few things less. Everyone appeared engrossed in conversation, yet they fell apart spontaneously as Sir Llew proceeded on his way like a modern day Moses.

In a cosy corner sat the multimillionaire entrepreneur, Christopher Freeman, with a captive audience all around him. Late forties, not tall, almost slight, but dapper in his expensive evening clothes. Freeman was extremely attractive in a dissipated kind of way, with thick fair hair and razor-sharp grey-blue eyes.

A woman of uncertain age was sitting beside him on the brocade-covered sofa, intimidatingly glamorous, regarding Chloe with an odd flicker of hostility. Chloe didn't quite know why.

She was to find out.

From the very beginning Christopher Freeman had been a cradle snatcher. Introductions were exchanged. McGuire said something quite witty about their earlier encounter, which Freeman, too rich to care about what anyone thought, appreciated. Both Chloe and McGuire were invited to join the charmed circle.

"Just try to look intelligent, my dear." The ruthless woman smiled more tolerantly at Chloe, obviously thinking she and McGuire were a couple and Chloe probably wouldn't get the point of anything that was said.

It wasn't the case. Though Chloe didn't put herself forward, she was well able to take part in a discussion which included world politics, a few jokes and a lot of gossip. It lasted almost half an hour before McGuire, smooth as you please, just as he would close a staff meeting, extricated them from the great man's side.

"God, he hasn't changed a bit," McGuire said disgustedly. "The perfect promoter. Floater of deals."

"He was being very nice to you," Chloe ventured.

"And to you." McGuire's words were light, laconic, but a faint anger registered in his eyes.

"At least he liked the enlivening conversation. Most people must sit back open-mouthed and let him talk. It must come as a diversion to have someone like you around." McGuire had had no hesitation levelling a few criticisms at Freeman's views. Criticisms, Chloe had to admit, she agreed with. Christopher Freeman's world was money. Exclusively. He had lost all touch with the man in the street.

At different stages of the evening, Chloe found Freeman at her shoulder, obviously keen to enjoy her company. Although it was flattering in a way, Chloe was beginning to feel uncomfortable with the way his eyes continually rested on her mouth. Was he one of those people who liked to lip read or had he something else on his mind?

McGuire apparently thought so because he wasted no time drawing Chloe aside. "It might be a good idea if you stick with me for the rest of the evening, Chloe," he suggested. They were alone on the terrace, which was cool and quiet.

"Wouldn't that cramp Tara's style?" she asked rather mischievously, only McGuire continued to gaze at her in exasperation.

"With a man like that, you don't need to give an inch."

Play it cool, Chloe thought. He is your boss even if you don't heed the lecture. "Gabriel, if you think I'm interested in Christopher Freeman you're completely out of your mind," she said sweetly.

He waved that away. "But he's interested in *you*. He likes nothing better than the chase, then the takeover."

Chloe's voice carried a trace of the redhead's volatile temper. "Listen, I appreciate your concern, Gabriel, but let's get one thing straight. I can look after myself."

"Not so I've noticed," McGuire replied unforgivably. "Freeman has an ego the size of Centre Point tower. You might well find he'll refuse to believe you're not equally attracted."

Chloe's deep blue eyes sparkled. "Despite the fact he's old enough to be my father?" She looked up into McGuire's face, which to her surprise suddenly appeared strikingly handsome. It certainly fared much better than Freeman's in every regard.

"Chloe." He sighed heavily. "That's no comfort to me. Men as rich as Freeman generally get what they want. He makes no secret of the fact, the younger the better."

Clearly he was sincere, so Chloe spoke more gently. "Gabriel, please allow me to take my own chances. You're overreacting, which is very unlike you."

"Well, I'm going to pray that you're right." He looked down at her, saw the same thing Freeman was seeing, a ravishingly pretty, highly desirable young woman, only in his case he knew when to hold back. He didn't believe Freeman did. "I've had this little voice in my ear all night," he confided. "Very, very odd. Like a counsellor. I know Freeman from way back. He's a lot trickier than a young woman of your limited experience can imagine." The instant he said it he felt a sharp little twinge, like someone had pinched him. He even winced.

"Limited experience?" Chloe tilted her chin. Was he telling her he knew she had never had a passionate love affair in her life?

"I think you know what I mean," he said, watching the colour roll over her beautiful skin.

"No, I don't. Tell me about it," she invited, stepping a little closer to his very much taller and heavier figure.

"Chloe, we're not going to have an argument here, surely?" He had to smile at the light of battle in her eyes.

"Too right. You came as my boss, not my minder. I don't need you to watch me like a hawk."

But she does.

It was that voice again, thoroughly unsettling him. A sweet pure voice. Like the voice of a boy soprano. McGuire hit his head none too lightly with his hand. He'd been working very hard lately. Long hours. Too little sleep. Maybe he was going ga-ga.

"What is it, what's the matter?" Chloe was bewildered. "You're all right, aren't you?"

He stopped abruptly. "What do you call that ringing in the ears?"

Chloe stared at him in consternation. "Tinni... tinni..." She searched her brain. "Tinnitus. Ringing in the ears. Is that what you've got?"

"Must be," he said laconically. "I don't think it's as serious as schizophrenia."

"Gabriel." She found herself troubled. She reached out and clasped his hand.

The sweetness of the gesture entranced him, gave balm to his genuinely unsettled feelings. His smile was very white. "I'm okay, of course I am. Let's go inside, shall we? I can see supper is being served and I have absolutely no intention of handing you over to Freeman."

That should have been the end of it, only Tara shamelessly suggested to Christopher he had made a conquest which Freeman the egotist complacently accepted. He was, however, a mite surprised. Chloe Cavanagh was a beautiful and interesting young woman but he hadn't detected any of the usual signs. Moreover she had the big fellow McGuire constantly at her side. A man to be reckoned with, Freeman knew intuitively. As a journalist McGuire had been first rate, maybe too straight to go down well; too unrelenting in the quest of the truth. He didn't put a great deal of faith in what Tara Williams had to say, either. It was abundantly clear she had the hots for McGuire.

The instant Tara succeeded in detaching McGuire from Chloe's side, Freeman walked towards her, this time his manner a touch more courteous, impersonal. He knew a class act when he saw one.

She lapped it up, he thought, visibly relaxing. They got to chatting about—of all things—his life. How he had adored his mother, hated his father, how he had done very badly at school because he was sick of listening to stupid teachers' ramblings, his first big break, his first million at twenty-four, his first marriage, a jolly girl but she couldn't take the pace, his love affair with the United States. He didn't really notice it, but he was being interviewed. Chloe talked little, inserting key questions from time to time. He was charmed.

Across the room, Tara was rapturous at having Gabe to herself. She found him intensely sexy, so big and powerful, wonderful to talk to, a touch spiky, with a rather formidable aloof core that nevertheless made him more interesting. She had wanted him from their very first meeting when her father had invited him home to dinner, though it had become abundantly clear she would have to work hard to land him, which was her quest. Most of her friends were already married, or at least engaged. She wasn't going to allow Gabe McGuire to get away. She *couldn't*.

For his part, Gabe realised with increasing irritation he wasn't enjoying this party at all. Every time he turned his head he could see Chloe's lovely profile etched against the light from a nearby lamp. Opposite her, knees almost touching, was Freeman talking non-stop, smiling, animated, confident, immensely comfortable with this slip of a girl. Chloe was wonderful as an interviewer, McGuire thought ironically. Maybe she was after a story? Freeman so far as he was concerned had had an entirely different agenda.

Why don't you take her home? someone whispered in his ear.

"I don't know that she'll want to come," Gabe replied in amazement.

"What was that, old chap?" one of the guests turned around smilingly to ask.

Goodness, had he spoken out loud? "Sorry. Just talking to myself."

"I do it all the time." The man smiled indulgently.

Nevertheless Gabe was rattled. Who *exactly* was it who was talking to him? Not that it wasn't good advice and he should act on it. Gabe glanced at his watch. Well after midnight. No doubt the party would see the light of day, but he felt it wasn't an unreasonable time to leave.

Both Freeman and Chloe looked up at his approach.

McGuire was so physically impressive, Freeman at five foot eight, he always said five-ten, felt an almost unbearable stab of envy. "Dare I break up this little chat?" McGuire sounded light-hearted, amused, when his black, black eyes said something entirely different to Chloe. "I'm about to say my goodbyes, Chloe, if you're coming with me."

Chloe, knowing McGuire, knew she didn't have a lot of choice. She looked across at Freeman with a gentle, charming smile. "Gabriel has been kind enough to offer me a lift home."

"Couldn't you stay?" Freeman asked, looking vastly put out. "I mean, I'd be delighted to drive you home. I have a limousine on call."

Chloe was aware of McGuire's brilliant dark gaze on her. "I've had a lovely time," she said, when she really hadn't, "but finally I must go. It was wonderful talking to you." Chloe stood up and Freeman did too. "Well, good night." She gave him her hand.

"But I must see you again." He looked his consternation.

"We keep her pretty busy at BTQ8," McGuire came back.

"You've been so kind, I can't tell you," Chloe murmured, conscious of McGuire's towering figure.

"Well, I could come on your station," Freeman drawled enticingly.

"We haven't got that kind of money," McGuire said with one of his biting smiles.

"I'll do it for free if only Chloe interviews me," Freeman said. "And I have proper control, of course, not that I don't trust Miss Cavanagh."

"I'm sure it would lift the ratings," Chloe couldn't resist saying. These days Christopher Freeman was almost impossible to get to.

"So it's a deal?" Freeman gave Gabe a cool smile.

"I'm more than happy with it," Gabe lied. "I'll phone you Monday, if that's okay?"

"I insist on taking you and Chloe to lunch." Freeman could see he wasn't going to get rid of McGuire so easily. It was on his face.

"Fine."

"Interviewing Christopher Freeman on 'Lateline.' I can't believe it!" Chloe said as they left the Williams' mansion well over twenty minutes later. Tara had kissed McGuire goodbye quite blatantly on the mouth, ignoring Chloe totally.

"No need to go wild." There was a slight edginess in McGuire's deep attractive voice.

"Heck," Chloe said. "You don't mind, do you? It's quite a coup."

"I agree, but is it *worth* it?"

"Anyone would think I was about to fall in love with him."

McGuire's expression was mocking. "Most women would be very happy to marry a billionaire."

"I'm afraid you're right, but I don't happen to be one of them. The only person I'd get into bed with is the man I love."

"Have you met him or are you still looking?"

Chloe moved back in the plush leather seat. "There must be *some* lovely men out there. Most I meet are totally unsuitable."

"I expect that includes me." He glanced at her with open challenge.

"Actually, no. Isn't that strange? In many ways you impress me very much."

"I think you're lovely, too." He looked over at her and gave a sardonic smile.

As the car pulled up outside Chloe's house, she found herself flooded by sensations so unfamiliar she actually started to stammer. "Th-thank, thank you, so much, Gabriel, for going out of your way."

He looked at her with a mixture of amusement and indulgence. "I've loved every minute we managed to be together."

"Honestly, you're dreadfully sarcastic." She was quick to open the door.

"I generally mean what I say, Chloe. Hang on, I'll come around. I have every intention of seeing you to your door, maybe waiting while you check out the house. One can't be too careful these days."

"Gabriel, don't be ridiculous." She was feeling more and more shaken by the minute.

He took her hand. "Do me the kindness of easing my mind."

"But I'm in and out of the house all the time." The last thing she needed was for Gabriel McGuire to turn his intense energies on her, let alone look at her with any kind of raw emotion. Talking to Christopher Freeman had been a piece of cake, dealing with McGuire was and always had been acutely disturbing. Even this one evening had accelerated their odd relationship.

At the door he took the key from her, let them into the house while he waited for her to do a quick inspection of all the rooms. He even walked around himself, peering behind doors, lifting out curtains, turning on the switches to floodlight the rear garden.

"Why don't you get a dog? A German shepherd?" His gaze scrolled the backyard.

"And what does the poor thing do all day and half the night when I'm away?"

He sighed, looking broodingly handsome. "No, that wouldn't work." He turned off the exterior lights. "It's getting late. I'd better go."

"Yes." She had thought about offering him coffee and rejected it on the basis there was too much prickly excitement. "Thank you again."

"What are you doing tomorrow?" he asked unexpectedly, walking towards her.

Chloe took a very deep breath. "I have lots of household chores to catch up on. Then I visit my mother."

He nodded, looking down at her with quiet approval. "You must love her very much?"

"I do." For a second her eyes glistened.

At the front door he turned. "Let me handle Freeman, Chloe."

"It's *me* he wants to talk to," she said impishly.

"Lord, yes. His interest was very apparent to us all. Well, good night then."

"Good night, Gabriel." She looked up at him, feeling a tremendous rush of the underlying attraction she sought so valiantly to hide. She acknowledged it for a single moment in her eyes.

"It's so rare of you to smile at me like that." He turned her face up to his, scanning the small classic features, the alluring full mouth, reading the blue eyes that flickered her myriad thoughts. Then he bent his dark head and kissed her.

It was brief, so brief, yet she felt the throb of it right through her body. On her mouth, in her throat, in her breasts, deep in the pit of her stomach, tingling down the length of her legs.

When it was over she looked up at him speechlessly, for once in her life deprived of words.

"Sleep well, Chloe," he said. "May your guardian angel watch over you."

Then he was gone, loping down the short flight of steps, along the ungravelled drive, out onto the quiet tree-lined street without once looking back.

That was a kiss women would die for, Chloe marvelled as she fumbled several times to lock the front door. And from a man she had long viewed with a mixture of hostility and awe. She had always known at some point McGuire would shock her. From now on she would have to keep a very careful eye on that dangerously complicated and complex man.

CHAPTER THREE

SUNDAY morning Chloe awoke with a tremendous start. The doorbell was ringing. A glance at her bedside clock told her it was almost nine-thirty. She had slept in, a rare luxury. She staggered out of bed, threw on a robe and padded to the front door, holding her riotously curling hair out of her eyes.

A young man stood on the verandah holding the biggest floral arrangement Chloe had ever seen outside society weddings, gala dinners and the like. There were masses of flowers, roses, carnations, lilies, orchids, clouds of baby's breath, exquisite foliage all wondrously put together in a large white wicker basket.

"Miss Chloe Cavanagh?" Who could mistake her or that fabulous red hair?

Chloe stared in amazement. "Somebody has made a mistake." These were flowers for a hospital; flowers to make a patient's day.

"I don't think so." The young man smiled, moving the arrangement fractionally so she could now see the logo of a well-known nursery that also specialised in the cut flower trade, on his pocket. "One-twenty-one Sunderland Avenue."

"I didn't think anyone delivered on a Sunday." She wobbled a little as she took the full weight of the arrangement.

"We do if it's worth our while. That's some arrangement you've got there." He grinned.

Inside the house Chloe pondered what to do with it. The library table was the obvious place but she rather liked her own bowl of roses. The basket was too heavy

61

to hold, so temporarily, she set it down on the floor, reaching for the card that went with it.

"Thank you for a delightful evening. Christopher." Lord! She hoped he didn't expect her to ring around to find out where he was staying then put through a gushing thank-you call. Beautiful as they were, she simply didn't need this floral offering. It was too excessive, too expensive, and it imparted a message she didn't want to hear. In some things McGuire really did know best.

In the office Monday morning McGuire called her in, his manner very much back to business. The kiss they'd exchanged might very well have been something she dreamed up.

"I've lined up that luncheon with Freeman for Wednesday," he told her, waving her into a chair. "Keep the afternoon free, 1:00 p.m. at Michaels." He named the swishest restaurant in town. "I've also spoken to Sir Llew who's delighted Freeman will do it for us. Not out of the kindness of his heart as he at first volunteered. Top dollar. I've spoken to Gray, as well." Graham Hewett was the name of the top journalist who hosted the show. "It won't come as any surprise to you that a few people will have their noses put out of joint."

"I'm prepared for it," Chloe said.

He looked across the width of his desk at her, at her beauty which gave her such an advantage, unfair a lot of people thought, but it was allied to a keen intelligence and a very professional on-camera manner.

"You've come a long way in a short time," he said musingly.

"I hope you're happy for me?"

"As a matter of fact, I'm about to offer you a raise."

"Really?" Chloe was both surprised and delighted. "This might be the start of a good news week. Dare I ask how much?"

"I don't think you'll be disappointed." He named a figure that she found slightly staggering. It would ease some of her anxieties about keeping her mother on at the nursing home.

"That's very generous of you, Chief." She was back to the familiar form of address.

"I'm glad you feel that way, Cavanagh," he lightly mocked. "Anyway you're worth it to the station, providing someone doesn't break your pretty little neck," he finished more soberly.

Chloe didn't laugh. "We all take that chance."

"I know. The only trouble is there are more and more unhappy hurting people out there, ready to lash out at government, at the media. And always the ratbag to stir them up. I want your promise you'll show extra caution in all your assignments. I've already spoken to Bob." He considered for a moment, frowning. "Come to think of it, I might give you another cameraman."

That sounded an alarm. "Oh, no, Chief, Bob and I are a team."

"A team of short guys," he said bluntly. "Neither of you would clear five-four. Bob, quite frankly, is out of condition, as well. I'll swap him over with Giles Stockwell."

Chloe was dismayed. "Please, Chief, don't do anything like that. I promise I'll take all the necessary precautions. A bodyguard is not the answer. The couple of scrapes I've got into have been my fault. I admit it. I was hot on the story. Bob urged caution all along."

McGuire sighed. "All right. I'll go along with it for now, but I want to make it perfectly clear to you, back off from any situation that looks dicey. Times have changed, I'm afraid."

Chloe nodded. Indeed they had.

"By the way, the De Havilands are giving Freeman a little shindig up at their mountain eyrie this Sunday," he said without enthusiasm. "Quite a lot of people will be going. Freeman himself requested you come along, unless you've something better to do."

Chloe didn't answer for a minute. She looked up to find McGuire examining her intently. "You're not going to believe this but he sent me a basket of flowers yesterday so wide it was all I could do to get it through the front door."

"Why *wouldn't* I believe it?" he asked in a deep rumble.

"Well, I didn't think you credited him with being so romantic."

"Surely you're not entertaining the joyful hope he is?" he retorted quite sharply.

"If you *must* know, I took them out to the nursing home," Chloe relented.

"Didn't you resist the impulse to keep a single rose for yourself?"

"Chief, the whole purpose of my talking to Christopher Freeman was to get a story," Chloe said in a serious voice. "I accomplished that. I seem to recall he deeply resented *your* line of questioning when you were on the job."

"Resent Away is my motto."

"My only reason for following any of this up is *professional*," Chloe stressed, aware of his antagonism.

"Was I implying anything else?"

"I think so. Anyway, I visit my mother every Sunday without fail. What time are you talking?"

"It's open house." He shrugged. "The buffet will be open all day."

"Are *you* going?" she asked, thinking he was bound to be. Along with Sir Llew and the bold Tara.

"I've got to tell you, Cavanagh, I am," he drawled. "Does that make a difference?"

"Indeed it does," she said breezily. "I need the benefit of your presence to keep Freeman in line."

He gave a crooked smile. "Thank you for your honesty, Chloe. It's not that you want to spend the day with me?"

"No way," she said sweetly, tucking back a stray curl. "From what I saw of Tara Williams, you're taken."

"Don't talk rot," he said, looking broodingly handsome.

"I always let my instincts roll."

"What my Irish grandmother used to call a woman's intuition." He laughed.

"Exactly. I understand perfectly if you want to get going fairly early."

"No. I'd prefer the excuse to wait for you. What time could you leave?"

"About midday, something like that. I could stay with Mum for a few hours."

"Midday would be perfect. It'll take us a good hour to get up the mountain."

"I've heard it's a fabulous house."

"It is, but the view of the Glass House Mountains is even better." He hesitated, looking uncharacteristically uncertain. "I don't want to sound intrusive, but I'd welcome the opportunity to meet your mother."

"Gabriel!" She spoke his name, sounding very surprised and forlorn.

"I could pick you up around ten, take you to the nursing home. We could go on to the De Havilands' after that. It's on the way," he pointed out persuasively.

"You *do* know that my mother is in a waking dream state?" Chloe asked, pain in her dark blue eyes.

"Yes, Chloe, I do," he said gently. "I'm sure she won't object to a friend."

Chloe bent her head. "No," she said in a low voice.

She had no idea how he had come to be a friend, but he was. "She knows about you, anyway."

"Maybe I'm not so happy about that," he said with sardonic amusement. There had been plenty of times she had stalked out of the office maddened.

"I sit with her and hold her hand," Chloe said by way of explanation. "Push her wheelchair around the grounds. They're lovely. Especially at this time of the year when the jacarandas are about to burst into flower."

"Well, at least I can help you there," he said, his cynical heart melting at the still-blue light of tears that stood in her lovely eyes. She was breathing deeply to maintain her control, the pearly nacre of her teeth just visible between her parted lips. He remembered with anger how Freeman's rapt gaze had focused on Chloe's cushiony mouth the other evening. Not that he could blame him. Sometimes he had called her into his office for the sheer pleasure of looking at it. She would be wonderful to make love to. Wonderful to bring to full sensuous life. The child of a violent dysfunctional family, McGuire knew instinctively Chloe in an entirely different way had suffered damage.

The rest of the time they discussed assignments. The ones he knew Chloe could handle well, the ones he preferred to leave to other journalists. That afternoon she was to interview the novelist, Jake Wylie, with a view to a segment on "Lateline." Tomorrow there was Professor Sophie Gordan, the outspoken academic and defender of women's rights; one of the recipients of the recent Young Achievers awards, a brilliant young aboriginal artist, and Piers Edmiston, the visiting concert pianist and expatriate Australian.

McGuire looked up from his pad. "I almost forgot. I've had a call from the Turf Club. They particularly want you to present the Fashions on the Field awards at the Spring Carnival. 'You're so beautiful and friendly,'

I quote. Daniel Shepherd has offered to dress you. Does that appeal?"

"Absolutely!" Chloe gave him her heart-stopping smile. "I *love* his designs! I even bought one for a friend's wedding but not anymore. Too expensive."

"All free, Cavanagh. And free publicity for them. You should look ravishing. You might like to confirm things yourself." He handed her a slip of paper with names and telephone numbers on it. "We're upping your dress allowance, as well."

Chloe clutched at her heart. "You can't expect me to take this in all at once."

"You pay for dressing, Cavanagh," he told her. "The okay has come from the top. Sir Llew is impressed with you and he's notoriously hard to please."

"I bet you had something to do with it all the same," she said shrewdly.

He laughed briefly, mocking, self-derisive. "I'm a super guy, Chloe. Maybe you'll find that out."

At the last minute, because of work pressure, McGuire had to pull out of the midweek luncheon appointment with Christopher Freeman.

"Explain the circumstances, would you?" There was a faint, almost undetectable look of edginess on his face. He contemplated Chloe on the other side of his desk. She was beautifully turned out in a sugar pink suit that did wonderful things for her hair and her complexion. She even had a touch of the celestial, he thought, with her luminous aura and that pearly pink lipstick on her soft luscious mouth.

"Of course. I'm really sorry you're not coming," Chloe said. And she was.

"You sound like you actually mean that." His tone registered a sardonic surprise.

"I do."

He smiled at her, his expression half pleased, half ironic. "Are you sure you can put up with him on your own?"

"I think so. For someone so incredibly successful, I don't find him at all imposing." Not like you.

"You've never seen him doing business, Chloe," McGuire answered a little grimly. "He has a deserved reputation for being absolutely ruthless."

"He can be charming," Chloe offered mischievously, McGuire was looking so openly Big Brotherly.

"Just remember, he knows how to flatter women, he knows how to get them into his bed, what he doesn't know is how to *appreciate* them."

"Do you mean you do?" Chloe asked lightly, widening her blue eyes.

"Put it this way, Chloe," he rasped. "I feel strongly about the institution of marriage. When I do get married it will be for the long haul. Freeman tends to chop and change, if you've noticed."

"You're really a very intense person, aren't you," Chloe said, thinking that was true.

He gave her a sharp look of acknowledgment. "If the definition is 'feel deeply,' yes. I have expectations for the future, Cavanagh. They don't all relate to career possibilities as you seem to think. I want a wife and family. I want the role of husband and father. A wholeness in life."

"Then you'd better turn your attention to it," she retorted sweetly.

"Maybe I already have," he drawled. "As regards Freeman, all I'm doing is urging you to a certain wariness. Unfortunately Freeman has the capacity to cause harm. You'd be foolish if you didn't face it."

Chloe shook her radiant head. "I understand, Chief. You've no cause for concern. This luncheon is strictly on the job."

Freeman, of course, had a concealed agenda. To lure Chloe into his web.

"I'm sorry Gabe couldn't make it," he said when they met at the restaurant, his expression totally belying his words. "What a character he is!"

"He is that," Chloe agreed, feeling Freeman's hand at her elbow as the maître d' escorted them to their table.

The beautifully appointed riverside room was almost filled with people, many of whom looked up in recognition of the high-profile Freeman with the popular young TV personality Chloe Cavanagh in tow.

"I don't think it will take Gabe long to reach the very top," Freeman continued when they were seated beside the plate-glass window that overlooked the lovely tropical gardens and the esplanade. "Maybe even stealing Llew's job."

There was a certain malice to it, even a kind of envy. "I don't think McGuire's into *stealing*."

Freeman's smile was faintly rueful. "All right. All right. I understand loyalty to the boss."

"The loyalty is deserved." The words were sincere but Chloe kept her tone light. "McGuire works harder than anyone I've ever known. Not to mention putting the rest of us through our paces. I used to have quite a soft spot for my old boss but I've been forced to admit we were going nowhere until McGuire arrived."

"You call him McGuire, then?" Freeman sounded pleased.

"McGuire. Chief. He doesn't mind either."

"I thought you were calling him Gabriel the other night?"

Chloe smiled. "We agreed Christian names would sound better for the night."

"So there's no romance there?"

"Whatever made you think that?" Chloe asked, trying to puzzle out why he should think it.

"For the very good reason he exuded protectiveness. I wouldn't care to get on the wrong side of your charismatic friend."

"Isn't that a wee bit melodramatic?" Chloe asked lightly.

"Not at all. I've had a great deal of experience, Chloe. Gabe McGuire would make a dangerous enemy."

"It's a good thing, then, we're all on the same side."

The waiter arrived sometime later and took their order. Fresh-from-the-bay, steamed-in-the-shell scallops with ginger and spring onions for Freeman, tiny bay lobsters in a lime sauce for her, followed by the truly superb tropical fish, the barramundi cooked in the Asian way for her, with roast lamb with eggplant and zucchini ratatouille on couscous for him. Chloe declined dessert. Freeman thought he might well have that "wicked-looking chocolate torte on the trolley." Afterwards they fell into pleasant and easy conversation, with Freeman on his very best behaviour. This wasn't a rush job, he had seriously decided.

Consequently Chloe was back to the office much later than she intended, running into Jennifer Bourne, the station's senior woman journalist as she returned from a political rally; the Prime Minister in the hot seat.

Chloe didn't expect a friendly greeting. Jennifer had become increasingly hostile as Chloe climbed the network ladder.

"Hi, Jen!" Chloe called in a relaxed voice, walking faster to catch up. She hated all this bitterness in the air.

Jennifer, a tall, attractive brunette in her early thirties, turned around. "Ah, our little Chloe as immaculate as ever. Where have you been? Not on the job in that get-up?"

"Actually I've been out to lunch." Chloe didn't dare say with whom.

"That's amazing," Jennifer said acidly, glancing at

her watch; nearly four. "How do you manage to get around Gabe?"

"Boy, how many times *haven't I?*" Chloe retorted with feeling.

Jennifer brushed her response aside. "You had no one else to blame but yourself. You should have let someone else track down that criminal Ed Cleaver. I know Sir Llew wasn't happy about it. I wouldn't brave such a nasty piece of goods."

"All he did was threaten, Jen. He didn't do anything."

"Go on." Jennifer held up a hand. "He broke Bob's camera. An inch closer to you and he would have broken your pretty little nose."

"Jennifer, what's the matter?" Chloe asked gently. "We used to be friends."

Jennifer was silent for a moment, looking of a sudden faintly shamed. "Maybe you're having too much fun playing Gabe's little pet."

Chloe had to laugh. "How can you *say* that? You've been in on plenty of our spats."

"Just a smokescreen," Jennifer broke in. "Was I ever wrong about you. I realise now that you're all about tactics. The fiery little redhead who looks as fragile as a figurine. I saw you two together the other night at Sir Llew's party."

"You never spoke to me," Chloe said, still hurt. "Never came near me in fact."

"You were too busy latching on to Freeman."

"It was nothing like that, Jen," Chloe protested. "Freeman came after me."

"Why wouldn't he?" Jennifer cast a withering eye over Chloe's chic, petite figure. "Of course, I've got it. You're after an interview."

Chloe touched the older woman's arm. "Jen, there's

no use denying it. I'm a journalist just like you. Getting interviews with famous people is what it's all about.''

"Infamous, don't you mean?" Jennifer flashed back. "He might be a billionaire but a lot of people hate him."

"That goes with the territory. Can you think of anyone in that category who doesn't have lots of enemies?"

"Oh, let's keep walking," Jennifer said in an angry, frustrated voice. "Gabe doesn't do any pampering of me."

Chloe chose her words carefully. "You really like him, don't you?"

"I have great faith in him," Jennifer answered sharply. "He's brilliant. He's in this cutthroat business but he's got integrity. He has to take a lot from the top."

"I mean on a *personal* level," Chloe said.

Jennifer looked over Chloe's glowing head for a few seconds. "He'd never look at *me*. Sir Llew is doing his level best to throw Gabe and that nasty bitch of a daughter of his together."

Chloe shrugged. "Well, I've heard the gossip but he didn't seem too interested to me."

"You know as well as I do there are many ways to the top," Jennifer said harshly.

Chloe couldn't help it, she snorted. "I don't think you have to worry, Jen, Gabriel McGuire is going to make it on his own."

Chloe hadn't been at her desk more than fifteen minutes when she got a buzz from the man himself. McGuire's voice crackled with pent-up energy. "Do you think you'd better tell me why the hell you've been gone so long?"

"I'd love to, Chief," Chloe said with infuriating sweetness.

"Would two minutes in my office do?"

"Gotcha."

She was on her way out as her friend Mike Cole was

coming back in from covering a golf final. He held the outer door for her. "Hiya, Chloe. You look wonderful. Like a strawberry ice cream. Where have you been?"

She paused for a moment, winked. "Lunch with Christopher Freeman."

"No kidding?" Mike looked thrilled for her and vaguely alarmed. "I bet you had a time fending him off."

"He was a perfect gentleman, Mike. Besides, it's all on the job, an interview's been arranged. I'm off to report to the boss."

Mike laughed. "Is there a problem?"

"There's always a problem with McGuire."

"Only when you push him too far," Mike called after her. "Your goddaughter has been missing you. So has Teri."

"What about I call in early next week. I expect to be free."

"Make it tea."

"Great." Chloe waved back happily. She would confirm that with Teri, not that she had ever known a time however unannounced when Teri hadn't welcomed her with open arms.

"So how did it go?" McGuire wasted no time getting down to business.

"Did you know that Freeman is an insomniac?" Chloe said, dropping gracefully into a chair facing him.

McGuire's rugged dark face took on a saturnine cast.

"No, I know what you're thinking." Chloe laughed. "Aside from his love life, he rarely closes his eyes until around 4:00 a.m."

"Perhaps he's exaggerating a little, though I'm not much of a sleeper myself," McGuire said.

"Too many problems in life?"

"*You're* a problem, Cavanagh." His black eyes moved over her. "Anything else you found out or would you rather save it all up for the interview? Sorry to cramp your style but I'll vet your questions before you put them to him.''

"I don't propose to insult him," Chloe said brightly.

"What about the little barbs, Cavanagh?" he said with rich sarcasm. "You have been known to get them in."

"I'll get on the wrong side of Sir Llew if I offend his friend."

"Lord, yes." McGuire laughed a little bitterly. "It's been rather a long time since I did that. He hasn't forgotten."

Chloe thought she had found the perfect point. "Sir Llew never held it against you," she inserted deftly.

"My track record might be one of the reasons," he drawled. "Initially he opposed me."

That came as a surprise. Chloe shifted tack. "But you had the Big Guns onside?"

He nodded, cynically. "Unlike you, Sir Llew doesn't mix business with sentiment."

"That's a tilt at me, of course."

"You got it!" he jeered. "You were the one who liked to say I'd never fit into Clive's shoes."

Chloe's cheeks tinted a hot pink. "Well, I'm sorry. I was mistaken and that's that."

"No apology?" He kept his eyes pinned on her.

"I thought that's what *I'm sorry* meant."

"No way. Sorry doesn't begin to cover it. Anyway—" he shrugged the issue off "—what did you *eat?*"

Chloe heard the famished note in his voice. She even felt pressure on her shoulder, like her good fairy was giving her a nudge. "Gabriel, you've missed lunch." She sighed.

"What's new around here?" He flashed her a wry smile.

"Why don't I slip down the road and get Spiro's Deli to make you up some sandwiches?" she offered. "Some good coffee, too. I have a flask."

"Cavanagh, you'd do that for me?" His mouth curved up slightly.

"Unless we send Rosie," she joked. "No, I'm feeling quite the Good Samaritan. I'll go immediately. What do you want?"

"Listen," McGuire started, "I don't—"

"Allow me to do it for you. I bet you haven't had anything since breakfast."

"If you call breakfast an apple and a banana on the run," he said with a light mocking tone. "I don't have to send *you*, Chloe."

Chloe stood up. "I'm on my way."

At least she tried, but the moment she entered the foyer a powerful thuggish-looking man about forty with deep-set eyes and a sawn-off hairdo, hustled in the door.

"Hi, there, girlie," he bellowed.

The effect was electric. Amanda on reception shot up like her chair was on fire. "You want someone?" she croaked.

The thug ignored her, concentrating his attention to Chloe. "Ah, the little lady reporter." He patted himself on the chest for being so clever. "It's got nuthin' to do with you. Aren't *you* lucky."

"Who is it you're wanting? I might be able to help you." Chloe did a good job of covering her own alarm. This was one scary individual. She put her hand behind her back, trying to give Amanda a signal she hoped the normally bubbly receptionist would act on. There was a panic button situated just under Amanda's desk.

"Sure." The man sneered. "You want me to get tossed out of here, right? I understand that a reporter mate of yours, Bart Taylor, has been making a *lot* of people uncomfortable."

Chloe kept her expression calm. Bart had been investigating the drug scene and he was a very good reporter. "And what's *your* name?" Chloe asked. Something like Crusher, no doubt.

"That's you lot all over," the man said nastily. "Pokin' your noses into things that don't concern you."

"We're the media, aren't we?" Chloe challenged. "If you'll sit down I'll get someone to listen to your complaint. You're here to complain?"

"That's correct, girlie. Why not to you, now you're here. You're never off the television."

"I don't have the authority to speak for management." Where was security? Any other time you'd have to struggle to get past them. "Wait there and I'll get someone."

Chloe made to move off, only the man reached out and grabbed her arm.

"Hold it right there, girlie."

Chloe's whole body tensed. Was there ever a time she wasn't going to be called "girlie," she thought briefly. Amanda, who had never been confronted by such a situation, still stood immobilised but when the man pulled Chloe in front of him like a shield, Amanda let out peal after peal of shrieks from some inner reservoir.

Crusher was instantly outraged. "Shut up," he exploded as though he was the only one entitled to do any yelling. But Amanda, once started, was impossible to stop. She kept up a continuous shrill, keening like an attack-trained fox terrier, her pretty young face flushed a hot pink. There was a commotion in the corridor. A female voice began to shout incomprehensibly, then McGuire was pushing through, a towering presence with an expression of absolute disgust on his dark glowering face. Why was Cavanagh always in the thick of things? And why was Amanda shrieking like a bat out of hell?

"What the hell goes on here?" he demanded.

"Amanda shut up. *You*—" he addressed Crusher "—would you like to let go of my staff member." His voice vibrated with such anger even Chloe felt a cold chill. "Chloe, get over here."

Crusher who had lived all his life in a tough environment, knew when to give way. He let go of Chloe, abruptly giving her a little push towards McGuire who fielded her like a football, then sent her on a surging pass down the corridor where she was caught by a staff member who found the whole thing incredible. Someone else, Bob, was crawling on his hands and knees to get to the panic button behind Amanda's desk.

"Hold it, buster," Crusher yelled.

"Do what he says, Bob. Everything's fine."

"Where's Taylor?" Crusher demanded of McGuire, losing interest in Bob.

"I take it you've got some kind of beef," McGuire answered in a very tough voice indeed. "Just what *is* your problem," he barked.

Crusher all but crossed his eyes. "You don't know what's goin' to happen if Roberts keeps asking questions," he muttered with a kind of anguish. "They'll take it out on me." His gaze shifted to Bob, who was showing signs of heroism. "I told you to hold it. I gotta gun."

No! God, no! McGuire thought. This nut could turn out to be a walking time bomb. "Why would you be such a fool?" he rasped. "There are security guards on the premises and a patrol car on the way." Want to hear a joke, he thought bitterly. The security guards were probably enjoying a long, leisurely afternoon tea.

"I've got nothin' to lose," Crusher said pitifully. "That investigation has turned me into a fugitive."

It's clear I have to tackle him, McGuire thought. Security wasn't coming to the rescue. The fellow was big, hard, powerful-looking and obviously mixed up in the drug scene, but he'd faced worse. For some reason McGuire didn't see him as a killer. He didn't believe, either, he was armed, but maybe he was high on drugs. The man's body was starting to tremble violently. McGuire decided to change tack, instinctively listening to the little voice that started up in his head. "I wish I could help you," he said more kindly. "Investigations can be painful to a lot of people. On the other hand, I'm not going to do anything until you hand over your weapon."

"My life's been hell, man," Crusher responded to a hint of kindness.

"Why don't you go to the police? Ask for protection."

"They'd find me." Crusher's voice broke with emotion.

"You've spent time in jail?"

"Plenty." Incredibly he presented a proud grin.

"What state was this? Where? Queensland? New South Wales?"

All the time McGuire was talking he waited for the moment when he could safely take this man down, only a small figure in pink came hurling through the door like a guided missile, slamming into Crusher's back with the force of a runaway truck. Crusher grunted in pain, turning his head in utter confusion to see that pipsqueak girl. How could she possibly pummel so hard? She must have spent time in bad company.

It was all McGuire needed. While Crusher was so diverted, McGuire took him down in a first-class rugby tackle. Crusher hit his head on the tiled floor and passed out like a light.

At this point Bob reared up, ran to the panic button and pushed it.

"That's *my* job," Amanda snapped amazingly.

"For God's sake, Chloe." McGuire looked up at her,

his rugged face almost blank with disbelief. "I've never asked before, but are you doing weights?"

"The element of surprise, Chief." Chloe was trying to act casual. She had no idea what was happening to her. She wasn't on steroids. It was just like that other time. She assumed *powers*.

In the corridor quite a crowd had gathered, each with a different account, parting for the two security guards who now decided to push through into the reception area, looking mightily alert.

"What took you so long?" McGuire rasped.

"Sorry, sir. Sorry, Mr. McGuire," the two men blurted in unison. They sprang towards the groaning man on the floor.

"You'd better check him for a weapon," McGuire advised. "He said he was armed. I don't believe it myself."

"He isn't," Chloe said.

"And how would *you* know?" McGuire was grimly amused.

"I'm pretty sure, Chief. Poor devil's a basket case."

"And not only *him*."

"He's clean, Mr. McGuire," one of the guards confirmed, finishing his search and handcuffing the man's hands behind his back. Outside the building, the sound of a police siren rent the clear air.

"You okay, Chief?" Chloe asked.

McGuire momentarily lowered his dark head into his hands. "Sure. I just like sitting on the floor."

"Need a hand up?"

"I'm almost sure you could do it, which is ridiculous." He looked up into her lovely delicate face.

"A job worth doing is worth doing well." Chloe put out her hand and McGuire took it, fixing her with a mocking look.

She couldn't budge him. No way. There wasn't even

a suggestion of her former power. Instead he pulled her down into his arms.

"You're weird, Cavanagh. Do you know that?"

"I can't help it," Chloe said, with not the slightest desire to pull away.

By now the reception area was filled with people and Bob was happily videoing away for all he was worth. McGuire looked like a man who could handle any situation, but Chloe, locked in his arms, didn't look like she could be a threat to anyone past their tenth birthday.

How very deceptive appearances could be.

Amanda, almost fully recovered, had an admiring little group around her when two burly-looking policemen bustled in the front door.

"Right. Who's in charge here?" One of the policemen called in a loud voice.

"Why you are, Cavanagh, who could doubt it?" McGuire murmured, lifting Chloe and himself to their feet. "Gabe McGuire," he identified himself to the older police officer. "I'm the station manager."

"Can we clear this lobby? There are too many people milling 'round if you ask me."

The younger policeman took hold of the prisoner's grubby shirt and hauled him to his feet. "Gee, Blocker, can't you ever keep out of trouble?"

Crusher, properly identified as Blocker, glared balefully. "I didn't do nuthin', I only came here to talk."

"Well, you can talk at the police station, it's only a couple of streets away."

"Take him out into the car," his senior ordered. "I'll get a statement from McGuire here."

"Right, back to work." McGuire raised his voice only marginally, but it had its effect. "Do you want to come through to my office?" he invited the burly policeman.

"No, that's okay. You can tell me here." He placed his booted foot on top of a chair. "Miss Chloe

Cavanagh, right?'' Lord, she was cute. He couldn't wait to tell the wife. She always watched Chloe Cavanagh on the telly.

"Yes.'' Chloe smiled. "I was actually first on the scene.''

"Mind telling me everything that happened?''

"Not at all,'' Chloe said in her professional voice, then launched into a full account of the afternoon's events from the moment Blocker came through the door, how McGuire intervened, how he rescued her, how she tore through the back part of the building after McGuire pushed her out of harm's way, how she took up a position outside the front door within hearing but out of sight, waiting for the precise moment when she could bound in and divert Blocker for a few moments while McGuire did the rest. "I saw us as a team,'' she said, moving her head so she could read the policeman's notes better.

"Really?'' His steely gaze had softened miraculously. "I guess she's a lot stronger than she looks.''

"I studied ballet for about eight years,'' Chloe said modestly.

"Of course she did!'' McGuire seconded staunchly.

If I start to open up about my powers, someone might recommend me to a psychiatrist, Chloe thought.

About ten minutes later the police were ready to leave. "What's going to happen to him?'' Chloe asked her newfound friend.

"If he's smart he'll start cooperating with us and we can get to the root of why he came to the station,'' Senior Constable Drummond said. "Neither of you seemed too perturbed he just *might* have had a gun?''

Chloe didn't trust herself to answer.

"He just didn't sound at all convincing,'' McGuire said. "He was distraught, not violent. I took comfort from that.''

"Well, that should cover it, I guess." Constable Drummond slapped his notebook shut. "We'll let you know what happens next. Personally, I wouldn't want to cross you two."

"Like what happened to my sandwiches?" McGuire asked the moment the police had gone, his expression deadpan.

"I had a choice!" Chloe smiled. "Save you or take up a more strategic position at Spiro's Deli."

"You're crazy," he said for maybe the third time.

"Not really. You only need cheering up."

His dark eyes brightened. "I keep thinking I need to get something to eat. I could, of course, hang on if dinner wouldn't ruin your figure."

For a minute Chloe couldn't take it in. "You're asking *me* to dinner?"

"Something like that." He shrugged. "Just the two of us. No witnesses. I know I'm taking my chances just being with you."

"You mean you might be in danger?" This feeling of excitement was becoming increasingly familiar.

"It seems to be a regular part of your day."

"We survived."

"Sometimes I think it's because you're getting a bit of help." He gave her a wry smile.

"Where would we go?" Chloe asked, suddenly feeling marvellous.

"Let that be my surprise. Go home now. I'll pick you up around eight. I won't be able to get away before then."

Her eyebrows rose. "I thought I had to do the responsible thing and finish my day like everyone else."

"I'm sending Amanda home, too," he pointed out reasonably. "I'm sorry I barked at her but that shrieking wasn't something you'd like to hear every day."

"Poor Amanda!" Chloe sighed. "She'll jump at everyone who comes through the door now."

"Given that it has never happened before, she might settle down. On the other hand, she appeared to enjoy her fifteen minutes of fame. Now do what I tell you for once and take yourself off."

Chloe stared up at him, a little frown between her delicate brows. "I don't know why I *ever* thought I didn't like you," she said.

His brilliant eyes were deliberately sheened with challenge. "Let's see if *liking* is as good as it gets."

It was a taunt, she knew, and it brought a soft flush of colour back to her cheeks.

CHAPTER FOUR

THE restaurant McGuire chose was on the beautiful island-enclosed bay some thirty kilometres from the city. The great expanse of water was all ashimmer, filled with the reflected dazzle of the moon and the stars. Midweek the place wasn't crowded so they sat out on the wide, cool verandah enjoying the music of the palms that swayed along the foreshore and the fresh clean tang of the salt air as it blew in from the sea.

McGuire had ordered a lovely wine as soon as they arrived, now they sat sipping it from voluptuous long-stemmed glasses. He must have found time to nip back to his apartment, Chloe thought, watching the golden play of candlelight over his deeply indented chin. His was the kind of dark olive skin that quickly showed a swashbuckling beard, but he had obviously shaved, showered and changed his city clothes for smart casual with a whole lot of dash. In all fairness she had always admired his dress sense even as she wondered from whence it had come. Now it made her feel like a terrible snob. She herself had spent time choosing her short slip dress in a dusky shade of lilac crepe. It was beautifully cool. Perfect for such a glorious summer night. Had she known they were going to go bayside she would have worn a hibiscus behind her ear. Something about McGuire brought out an earthy streak in her. One could even call it sensual.

At any rate they both ordered oysters.

Chloe for her part scarcely knew what she was doing. It seemed impossible to believe she was here enjoying herself with Gabriel McGuire. She had always been so wary of him, fearful in a way, yet she had begun to relax the minute he had picked her up in the car. Maybe it was the wonderful cocoon effect of the Jaguar. She hadn't realised he was so witty, either. She knew he was remarkably well informed as she had to be herself. That was their job. Keeping abreast of what was happening all around the world, but frequently she found herself bursting out laughing at something he said while he looked back at her with black mocking eyes. She who had done so little to make him feel wanted let alone appreciated.

Of course they had to order seafood in an area celebrated for its marine bounty. Mountains of indulgence; tiger prawns, mouth-watering crab, scallops, baby lobster, calamari, perfect little fillets of catch of the day, all served on a large, colourful platter with a crisp and crunchy salad and tiny freshly baked rolls with a generous sprinkle of poppy or sesame seeds. McGuire with his much greater height and body size was still eating long after Chloe had stopped.

"Believe it or not," he said, "I'm going to have dessert."

"Go right ahead," Chloe encouraged him. "That was absolutely delicious but I couldn't manage another morsel. The food is wonderful here."

"We'll come again," he commented casually.

"You're going to ask me?"

"I was always going to ask you," he drawled, "I've just been waiting for the tiniest hint of a thaw."

Chloe cupped her hands around her flushed cheeks. "What really came between us?" she asked.

He gave her a hooded look. "I told you before, Chloe. Part of you doesn't want anyone getting too close."

"Maybe," she acknowledged, her blue eyes darkening. "And what about you, McGuire? You don't open up to anyone, either."

"I might to you."

There was such a depth to his voice she drew in her breath. "Then tell me about yourself *now*."

"What is it you want to know?" Suddenly his dark face assumed its brooding expression.

"We've had such a lovely evening, are you sure you want to be too serious?"

He reached out and briefly caught her hand. "Little one, I'm always serious," he said.

Whenever he touched her he made her heart pound. "Was your childhood really as bad as you intimated?" she asked, trying to keep her voice steady.

"Is this the start of an interview, Chloe?"

"No, Gabriel." She shook her head very seriously. "I'd really like to know."

"I don't know now that I ought to tell you." He was suddenly angry with himself. Why lay it on this innocent?

"It might help you." Chloe had the oddest sensation someone was at her shoulder. In fact she half turned to see who it was. No one, of course.

"Are you going to introduce a clinical note?" McGuire asked in a wry, sardonic tone.

"Don't be like that, Gabriel. I've acknowledged a few of my little hang-ups."

"Mine nearly crippled me," he said bluntly. "Growing up as you did in a beautiful environment with a loving mother and father, you could scarcely relate to *my* kind of background."

"Try me."

"I usually keep most of myself invisible," he said, then shrugged. "All right—my father was a Vietnam veteran. A helicopter pilot. He came home an entirely different person from the one who went away, my mother always said. All the pain that was locked inside him disrupted his whole life. And ours. My mother and me. Dad couldn't control natural aggressiveness that over the years grew into outright violence.''

"Oh, Gabriel, I'm sorry.'' Chloe leaned her head heavily on her hand.

"It happens, Chloe, over and over. Males are aggressive creatures right from the beginning. Most learn how to channel it, turn the drive into productive avenues.''

"*You* have,'' she said gently.

"Thanks, Chloe.'' His voice was dry. "But *you* have trouble with my image.''

She flushed a little. "Maybe the fault lies in me. I'm frightened of powerful emotions.'' Powerful men. "Can you understand that?''

He didn't answer for a moment, his eyes fixed on her, as beautiful as a dream. "Indeed I can. Actually I think you're very brave.''

"Goodness no!'' She remembered too well the awful times when she couldn't face the day.

"Your losses might have swamped anyone else.''

"Well, as you observed, Gabriel, I haven't got off scot-free.''

"Nor me.''

"You used the past tense when you were talking about your father.'' She picked up his story.

"He died, Chloe, prematurely. The only way he could live with himself was to drink.''

"And your mother?''

"She's okay.'' He shrugged. "Not good, but okay. She lives with her sister in Tasmania. I see her at least a couple of times a year. She always tries to tell me how sorry she is she wasn't stronger.''

"For you?'' Chloe could see how it might have been.

He nodded. "I was six foot at fourteen. It took two more years before my father discovered he was going to have to treat us in an entirely different way.''

"So your goals and your hopes are for a stable home life," she said sympathetically.

His expression was very deep. "I have a clear picture of peace and contentment, Chloe. Love and understanding within the family."

"I hope you find it, Gabriel," she said softly. "In fact I'm going to start praying for you this very night."

"I may need it." He sat forward, his powerful shoulders hunched a little.

"If you decide on Tara Williams," she responded a little more tartly than she had intended.

He laughed. "I like you when you're bitchy, Cavanagh."

"I'm not being bitchy." She didn't like to think she was. "Why are you looking at me like that?"

"All right, *jealous*," he jeered softly.

She groaned. "You fairly *amaze* me, McGuire."

"What have you got against Tara?" he asked, still amused.

It nettled her. "Heck, Gabriel, where have you been? She's terribly rude. She looks down her nose at everyone. She doesn't actually *do* anything, does she?"

"I've been told she does some social work occasionally."

"She's Sir Llew in a woman's body," Chloe said.

He considered that. "Maybe she is. A touch. But there's no doubt it's a marvellous body."

"You'd know, would you?" Chloe felt a sudden sense of heat.

"I believe I have *eyes*, Miss Cavanagh."

"I just want the best for you, Gabriel," she said simply.

"Well, at least that's cleared that up. Ready for coffee?"

"Why not."

It was when coffee was being served Tara Williams

and an escort, a big, overweight middle-aged man, flashily but expensively dressed, entered the restaurant. Tara was laughing merrily, drawing attention.

Chloe, facing the lobby, nearly fell off her seat.

"Lordy, Lordy, when was the last time you saw Tara?" she demanded.

McGuire didn't turn, unlike most people in the restaurant. "As in *Gone With the Wind?*"

"Second pick," Chloe said sharply.

"Tara Williams?" he guessed. "At the party."

"Well, don't look now but she's on her way over."

"Really? She has someone with her?" he asked mildly.

"Let me reassure you he couldn't compete with you in any way. Dark, balding, and decidedly overweight."

"That would be Al Jacobsen," McGuire said in a casual tone. "The real estate developer. He's in town."

"I hope you're all excited about meeting him," Chloe said. "They're being shown onto the verandah. I'd say directly past this table."

McGuire's expression was unconcerned. "I had a feeling they might be. Would you like to finish up that coffee?"

"Are you suggesting I gulp it down?" Chloe looked away. "I can make us coffee at home."

"Is that a promise?" One black eyebrow shot up.

"Nothing like that. Just a suggestion."

"Not very satisfying, Chloe." His black eyes glowed.

"All right then, a *promise.*"

A moment later Tara, looking startled, pointed her right arm dramatically. "Gabe, it can't be! Now here's a surprise." She turned back to her escort. "You've met Gabe McGuire haven't you, Al?"

"No," Al confessed, "I haven't. He smiled, displaying big strong white teeth.

Within minutes waiters were running in all directions

wondering if this was going to be a table for *four*. Even the soft clack of conversation inside the restaurant had stopped. Most people knew Chloe from the television, Tara Williams's face was equally familiar from the social pages, the two men were vaguely familiar, both exuding a languid, big-man authority.

Tara gave Chloe a cold, brilliant smile. A kind of I've-only-got-to-speak-to-Daddy-and-you're-fired smile. "I didn't know you and Gabe were friends?"

Chloe looked up, her tone gentle. "Now and again we call a truce. It doesn't last long."

The two men, as was men's wont, were shaking hands in a friendly fashion. McGuire, looking very tall and urbane, introduced Chloe.

"Maybe we can all have a drink together," Al Jacobsen suggested happily, while a waiter rocked back and forth on his heels waiting for a signal.

"Unfortunately, Al, Chloe and I have to drive back to the city," McGuire said smoothly.

Al considered that. "I know. It's easy to go over the limit. I've got a limo waiting outside."

"Well, its been nice meeting you, Al," McGuire said, shepherding Chloe into the aisle. "We'll leave you both to enjoy dinner. The seafood is wonderful here."

"So I understand," Al Jacobsen said, his deep-set dark eyes sparkling greedily. "Tara only discovered the place about a month ago."

"Didn't *we* come here, Gabe?" Tara asked with a neat blend of memory lapse and possessiveness.

"I can't take the credit, Tara," McGuire's expression was smooth and pleasant.

"I'm only in town for a week or two, Miss Cavanagh, but you can be sure I'll watch your show." Al stared down at Chloe with pleasure.

"She hasn't got a show." Tara wrapped her arms

around Al's sleeve. "Little segments, save the koalas, that sort of thing."

"'Little segments, save the koalas, that sort of thing,'" Chloe quietly fumed when they were safely inside the Jaguar and purring back to town. "I suppose, if Tara decided, I could get the bullet."

"Tara has *no* say," McGuire pointed out crisply.

"Are you sure of that?"

"They don't keep *you* on, Cavanagh, they don't keep *me* on."

Chloe turned to stare at his rugged profile. "You're joking, surely?" she asked cautiously.

"Chloe, you're what is known in the trade as a valuable piece of property."

"Ho!" Chloe sat back inhaling the rich leather. "That being so, I should be paid more for my services."

"You got a raise, didn't you," he countered.

"And I'm very appreciative of it, but Jana Wendt has asked for six million in compensation." Chloe named the most glamorous and powerful female presenter in the country currently at war with her station.

"Six million we cannot do," McGuire told her bluntly. "But you never know. You've got distinct possibilities. Possibilities you don't realise. What I want most of all, I've decided, is to get you in front of the camera."

"Hosting a show?" Chloe's smile bloomed.

"You're quite accomplished for one so young."

It was dreamlike, their harmony. Where is all this largesse coming from? she wondered. It was delightful and frightening all at the same time.

Back home Chloe sat McGuire down in the living room and went off to make coffee. A promise, was a promise, after all.

She was just about to carry it in when McGuire walked into the kitchen, instantly lessening the scale of the room.

"I got lonely out there," he complained.

"I could scramble you some eggs if you're hungry," she joked.

"I really enjoyed this evening, Chloe." His black gaze was locked on her. "I hope you did, too."

"There's a lot to be said for being friends," she pointed out lightly when all her pulses were aflutter.

"I'll have my coffee now, if you don't mind."

"Help yourself." She pushed his cup and saucer gently towards him. "Sugar, cream?"

"No, just black and strong. More than anything else I need a clear head."

She looked at him a little shocked. "We only shared a bottle, Gabriel."

"It's *you* I find intoxicating, Chloe," he said with more concern than ardour. "Are you going to sit down or are you going to hover like an angel?"

She not only felt like standing up. She felt like running. For McGuire to find her intoxicating? That was *stunning*. She could feel his magnetism, his male power all around her.

"I can give you an after-dinner mint with that," she managed.

"Sit down, Chloe, *please*," he begged. "I'm not about to grab you and press you to my manly chest. I've got a lot to think about."

"Like what?" Chloe asked faintly, slipping into a chair.

"We'll leave all that for a later date." He wasn't ready to explain. "This is good coffee."

"Supreme. I get it from Aromas."

"I love that dress, the colour. It sheens your eyes with lavender. You look beautiful."

"McGuire, I think you mean that," she said gently.

"Is there somebody floating around this kitchen?" he asked abruptly, looking up and around the ceiling.

Little ripples of sensation feathered around her skin. "As you said to *me* once, it's high time you got a good night's sleep."

"You don't feel some tender, solicitous presence?" he persisted, giving her the full battery of his black wonderful eyes.

She stared at him. "I didn't know you were religious, Gabriel."

"I haven't been, particularly up to date. Not that I don't *think* a lot." He sighed. "Bear with me for a while, Chloe."

"The truly odd thing is, I believe you. A few strange things have been happening to me, as you know."

"You're not lifting weights?" He attempted a joke. She was so feminine, so fragile, she took his breath away.

"No. You've put exactly how I've been feeling into words. A tender, solicitous presence."

"Every woman living alone needs that." McGuire looked across at her in her lovely lilac dress. From the moment he had laid eyes on her she had reminded him of something magical. A princess in a fable, sitting on a white unicorn, her long silky mane of red-gold hair flowing from under a high-peaked hat; those blue eyes and the slender graceful limbs. He supposed he was crazy about her but she needed nothing more than friendship and protection. She was far too precious for him. She had never known ugliness and fury.

"I suppose I'd better go," he said, rising instantly to his feet. "There's always an early morning start."

"I'll come with you to the door." Chloe sprang up like a deer, conscious of the powerful tide of feeling that swirled in him at some subterranean level.

He had a way of stalking ahead, of suddenly becoming preoccupied, so that Chloe, at his shoulder, bumped into him when he halted.

"God, I'm sorry." He gave her a hawklike scrutiny as though his tall, powerful body could have done her an injury.

"Really, I have to dance to keep up with you." She smiled.

Her smile was so soft, so sweet, he was entranced. "Good night, Chloe." His hand, large but beautifully shaped, grasped her gently beneath the chin. All would have been well, he only meant to kiss her briefly, a chaste salute, but Chloe at the last minute looked intently into his eyes. Into his *soul*.

He groaned. On a deeper level he moaned, his desire for her flaming out of bounds. He caught her to him, in his passion half lifting her off the floor, lowering his head in blind hunger, bringing his mouth down heavily over hers.

The effect was galvanic. The tender brutality of his kiss robbed Chloe of all breath. His physical strength was overwhelming, the fire that was in him. She had never been kissed so deeply, so voluptuously, in her whole life. Her whole body was quivering, quickening, clamouring. She was losing herself. Losing her shields and with them her defences. When his hand moved hungrily, tormentedly, over her breast she cried out as if in a mad ecstasy of panic, the blood glittering in her tight-stretched veins, silver shafts of pleasure piercing her very core.

He released her immediately, like an eagle shot to earth.

"I'm sorry, Chloe." His deep voice was startlingly harsh. He steadied her because she was swaying, nodded abruptly and strode to the front door.

Chloe hurried after him not at all sure what was happening. That *couldn't* have been a kind of self-disgust in his eyes? "I'm just fine. I was a little afraid for a moment."

"That's what I have to think about, Chloe." He turned back to her, his dark face taut. "You are indeed afraid of me."

"In a different way from what you think, Gabriel," she protested. For all his cleverness, his sardonic wit, she had hurt him. "You don't have to rush off like this."

"Oh, yes, I do. You bring me pain, Chloe, in some way. I suppose there's such radiance all around you."

She reached out, clasped his hand, bracing herself for his rejection. "I don't understand what's happening here."

"Oh, yes, you do, Chloe." He rejected her claim flatly.

"*Tell* me."

"You're not simple. You may be a virgin, don't ask me how I know, but I believe you recognise desire when you see it. I want you. I want you very badly. You've known it from the beginning. That's what makes you as nervous as hell."

"Gabriel, I'm a grown-up woman."

"That cry for help was genuine." His expression was grim.

Her face flamed. She dropped her startling blue eyes. "Maybe it was," she said in a subdued voice. "I've always done my best to stay clear of the rapids." She knew allowing Gabriel to make love to her would take her completely under.

"Maybe that's wise, Chloe." He gave her an odd smile. "Never mind, we can put the wall back up in the morning. See you." He sketched a brief military-type salute.

"You're still coming with me to visit my mother on Sunday?" she called as he opened the door to his car.

"If you want me to, Chloe."

"Of course I do."

Wave to him, a voice said. Wave him off.

She could *hear* the voice. It wasn't a voice in her head.

"All right," she said aloud. There was a lot of this sort of thing going about.

McGuire preparing to reverse out of the drive took one last look at Chloe, standing in her lilac dress, the exterior lights of the verandah making a glowing halo of her red-gold hair. She was waving so sweetly it all but eased the ferment that was in his heart. He waved back before he could prevent himself, distracted for a moment by a luminous patch of light that suddenly moved into his line of vision. It struck him it had an outline of maybe a small boy with some sort of white appendages he couldn't name. A trick of the light of course. Chloe obviously saw nothing by her side.

Even as McGuire continued to peer intently through the windscreen, sheened with salt, he now saw, the light changed, lost its extraordinary glow. He remembered all of a sudden what his mother used to say to him as a child.

"Gabriel, you have too much imagination."

Yet imagination was the key to wondrous new realms.

They saw little of one another for the rest of the week, though Chloe made a scoop, patched in live from the light aircraft terminal where an air traffic control officer was talking down a single engine Cessna. The pilot, a sixty-year-old grazier had suffered what his wife considered to be a heart attack and it was she who, with no actual experience save half a lifetime of flying with her husband, had to land the plane. It was a harrowing experience for all, Chloe feeding information to her channel, while everyone prayed for a miracle.

In the end the woman who had responded with the utmost courage managed to bring the plane down safely, after many terrifying kangaroo hops, to the resounding cheers of everyone at the airport.

Sunday morning Chloe was up early, dressed and waiting out on the verandah for McGuire when he arrived.

"Hi." She walked to the car, the morning sunlight firing her hair.

"How are you, Chloe?" He stood out on the driveway, looking, she realised, ruggedly handsome and devastatingly sexy, something she had always striven to ignore. But the time for all that was over, she thought fatalistically.

She smiled up at him, aware of a certain aloofness in his manner. "I'm fine. We stole Channel Nine's thunder with the airport piece."

"We did indeed." He held the door for her. "I heard late last night the husband is expected to pull through."

"Yes, I know. I called the hospital myself."

"You care, Chloe, don't you?" he said. "You don't walk away."

"I could never be so unfeeling." Chloe turned her head, saw the first time the large sheaf of pink roses on the back seat.

"For your mother," he said, slipping behind the wheel.

"That's very kind of you, Gabriel. They're lovely. Mum always loved flowers so much. I believe she still does."

"I'm sure." His expression softened.

"No phone call from Tara?" Chloe asked when he seemed predisposed to silence.

He eyed her somewhat coolly.

"I would have thought she'd be furious with you,"

Chloe found herself saying. Better a reaction, than no reaction.

"No use being furious with me." He shrugged, smoothly overtaking a slow-moving vehicle. "I don't take to it."

"But she *did* ring?"

"Heck, yes." He suddenly gave a quick, dashing grin. "I could do very well for myself there."

"Are you ambitious enough?" Something flashed in Chloe's blue eyes.

"I have to admit, Sir Llew is applying a little pressure."

"Is he? Isn't that disgusting?"

"You don't think I'd make a good match?" He flicked her a mocking glance.

"*You* were the one who spoke so eloquently about love."

"And you don't consider Tara lovable."

Chloe clicked her tongue and shook her head. "I don't know why I started this conversation."

"No, that's all right, Cavanagh," he said kindly. "Let there be no secrets between us. I can scarcely want you *and* Tara."

"Why me?" she asked, for some reason feeling like crying.

"Maybe the fact that you rejected me so completely made you that much more desirable."

"Is this true?" If so, it wasn't what she wanted to hear.

"No, it's nonsense. You took my breath the very first moment. I looked up and you were there. An angel come down to earth."

Chloe was moved. "Gabriel, that's the nicest compliment I've ever had in my life. I don't deserve it."

"No, you don't, you horrible little creature. You never show me any kindness or respect. It wasn't long before

I found out you were calling me a megalomaniac behind my back.''

"But a splendid megalomaniac, Gabriel. I always knew you were very clever.''

"Too late, Cavanagh. I'll pay you back one of these days. Remind me.''

They arrived at the nursing home a full ten minutes before time, taking the opportunity to walk around the extensive grounds. The magnificent shade trees, the jacarandas, had almost overnight burst into exquisite lavender blossom, all of them soaring to forty feet and more, colouring the tropical air mauve. Other lovely trees grew in the grounds, the purple and white orchid trees, the bauhinias that lined the perimeter and went so beautifully with the jacarandas. As the jacarandas turned back to dense feathery foliage the brilliant poincianas and the very old magnolias grandiflora would come into flower. Chloe had seen all the flowering in her time of visiting her mother.

McGuire was impressed. They were standing by the lake watching the play of sunshine over the dark green water. Numerous radiant insects were hovering over the lovely cream waterlilies cupped by large leaves and birds sang their delight in so beautiful a morning.

"Impossible to believe there's a lot of traffic out there.'' McGuire looked off towards the distant street. "It's so peaceful here.''

Chloe nodded. "It takes a lot of upkeep. There are quite a few groundsmen.''

"And I imagine it's expensive?''

"I may have to sell the house in time,'' she confided. "If Mum doesn't recover. But I feel if I did anything...'' She broke off unable to go on.

"I know what you mean, Chloe,'' he said simply.

Delia Cavanagh was sitting in her wheelchair, her back to them when they arrived. The light in the room was extraordinary, more silver than golden, clinging to her beautiful curly hair, shades lighter than Chloe's, more a bright copper, and to her soft blue robe.

"Good morning, Mumma," Chloe said, going to her mother and kissing her cheek. She turned the wheelchair. "I've brought someone to meet you. You've heard about him often. Gabriel McGuire."

Gabriel moved forward, holding the pink roses in one hand and taking Delia's fragile blue-veined hand with the other.

"Hello, Delia, I'm Gabe."

You have to get better, he thought, feeling a deep lunge of sympathy within him. Delia looked so completely peaceful yet she had slipped away from life. Understandable in a way. Chloe had told him her mother had adored her husband. Maybe this tremendous *hush* was Delia's choice.

Chloe, upset, took the flowers and set them down on the bedside table while her mother looked dreamily on, not registering Gabriel's presence by so much as the blink of an eyelid. Only while she was sitting there, her wheelchair bathed in a rainbow of sunlight, aquamarine, citrine, amethyst and garnet, like jewel colours seen through a prism, a change came over Delia Cavanagh; a spontaneous mental lift when for the space of a heart-beat she rediscovered happiness.

She *smiled*. A smile that lifted the corners of her mouth and showed in her eyes.

Chloe, the victim of countless crushed hopes, turned an anguished face to Gabriel. "She smiled, didn't she, Gabriel?" she begged of him.

Gabriel, stroking Delia's hand as if calling in healing power, couldn't bear her pain. "There's not the slightest doubt, Chloe." He felt he had witnessed not only Chloe's profound heartache but a moment of promise.

A minute but momentous *shift*.

"Come here to me." He put out his arm to Chloe, relieved beyond words when she came to him without hesitation, desperate for comfort. She was trembling, blue eyes glittering with standing tears.

"Mum has never smiled. Never once."

"She did then, Chloe." He couldn't bring himself to get her hopes up any further. But in his heart he felt there was a very slight possibility Delia Cavanagh could be coming back to wakefulness.

"Her doctors think she'll never recover."

But Gabriel had drawn reassurance from that smile. It was magical. "Doctors are sometimes wrong," he said carefully, even when the little flare of life, of intelligence, had died down in Delia as though she, too, conceded defeat.

"Maybe it's the drugs she's on. Maybe they are preventing her from—" Chloe broke off, a minute away from weeping. "Oh, God, I don't know."

It was cruel. Another hope dashed.

Yet there were vibrations in the room, vibrations far too subtle for the most powerful scanning device to measure. Vibrations that had entered Delia Cavanagh's body, beginning the work of lifting layer upon layer of miasmata.

By the time they were out in the beautiful grounds again, Chloe had stopped trembling. Gabriel was telling her mother a story about a trip he had made to Tibet, the Roof of the World. How he had been privileged to visit the Potala, the castle-like structure that was the private monastery of the Dalai Lama, where he and a few others had been granted an audience. He spoke of the Tibetan people, of the political situation, the religious rites, the prayer wheels and the awesome presence of the mighty snow-covered Himalayas. What was more extraordinary, Delia appeared to listen, her head cocked to one side like a bird.

Two hours passed during which time Delia seemed to focus on things around her, more specifically, her eyes were brighter, the gaze more concentrated.

Chloe did not trust what was happening. Life was cruel. She had good reason to know that. Maybe this was even an intimation her mother was about to leave her. That her father would come for her. Perhaps he was standing beside her at this moment. Someone certainly was. *Not* Gabriel. No one could miss Gabriel, so tall, so strong, so solidly *visible*. This was someone *unseen*. Someone who nevertheless breathed gently beside her. Hadn't she held her own breath many times trying to check where that other sound was coming from? When she was a child she had loved the idea of having her own guardian angel. A guardian angel to look after her. Where had he gone? And *who* had come back in his place?

Watching Gabriel so at ease with her mother, Chloe was overwhelmed by these moments of order. Moments of supreme clarity in the chaos of life.

The trip to the mountains refreshed Chloe's spirit. This was some of the finest scenery in the land. They drove past orchards and farming land, finally entering the fantasy landscape of the Glass House Mountains sighted by Captain Cook from the deck of the *Endeavour*. At that time a storm had passed over the rainforest and the steep volcanic tors had glittered like glass. As always the sight of Tibrogargan crouched above the mountain road made Chloe's heart leap into her throat. One came on it so suddenly; around a steep curve and it was there! Utterly *unreal*, like some prehistoric monster rising out of the thick scrub. Then as they followed the highway, climbing ever upwards, Tunbubalda, Beerburrum, Beerwah, and Coonowrin, soaring above the lush greenery. In these rich, red volcanic soils grew pineapples, avocados, papaws, bananas and all kinds of citrus fruit with fresh produce selling from roadside stalls at the entrance to the farms. This was lyrical country and Gabriel stopped the car on a hill high above one of the beautiful beaches with its white sand and rolling turquoise surf, to get the best view of the fantastic Dreamtime pinnacles, ranged side by side.

The De Haviland mountain sanctuary sat on a promontory overlooking the distant blue ocean with the rich hinterland in between.

"Isn't this exciting!" Chloe cried when the main house came into view.

"It has an Indonesian feel, don't you think?" McGuire, too, was impressed. "It blends so beautifully with the landscape. We've got the towering volcanoes, mercifully extinct, but where are the rice fields?"

Chloe laughed. "He's a brilliant architect. I read he and his wife spent a lot of time in Java."

"Actually she's Balinese. A beautiful, graceful creature. One up on you, Cavanagh."

"Really?" Chloe hadn't known.

The property was on luxuriant acreage with a profusion of tropical trees, plants and shrubs in flower, the combined scents pervading the blue and gold air. Cars were parked all over the grounds but McGuire managed to find a spot sandwiched between a Bentley and a very dusty four-wheel drive.

Their hostess appeared almost as soon as they arrived at the entranceway to what was really a complex of pavilions built on three levels. Dressed in a fuchsia silk shirt combined with royal-blue silk trousers and a vibrant pink sash, her long, gleaming black hair flowing down her back, Luna De Haviland was indeed beautiful with skin like a golden peach, and a wonderful welcoming smile.

"Please come in and meet everybody. Our guest of

honour hasn't as yet arrived,'' she told them with a twinkle.

The De Havilands had amassed the most wonderful things, Chloe thought as they followed their hostess through the main pavilion with its carved Javanese ceiling beams and ornate panels they learned later had been rescued from old buildings.

There were a lot of people scattered all over the rear of the main pavilion with its wonderful projecting deck that overlooked the breathtaking views. For a Sunday luncheon everyone was very glamorously dressed in expensive designer gear with lots of 18-carat gold; the women in a profusion of silk shirts of brilliant colours and patterns worn with toning skirts or trousers. Chloe herself wore pristine white, the fine lawn of her sleeveless shirt appliquéd down the front with seashells picked out in black and gold, a wide white and gold belt cinching her tiny waist, her linen trousers narrowly cut. Chloe knew exactly how to dress her petite figure, the resultant simplicity stealing a lot of the more spectacularly dressed's thunder. She was in fact earning herself something of a reputation as a trendsetter. Hence the invitation to cover the Fashions on the Field.

Their host, a very distinguished-looking man with prematurely grey hair, came towards them linking his arm with his wife's, introducing them both to the people they didn't know, the low-profile seriously rich. They waved and called hello to the rest, the high-profile society crowd. Since she had become a ''media figure'' Chloe had been invited to lots of places so she knew a lot of people. It was part of the job.

Almost immediately they were claimed by a smart young group, getting caught up in light-hearted conversation, until Tara Williams arrived in a skin-tight sleeveless black stretch top with caramel-coloured linen trousers and some kind of elaborate gold choker around her neck.

"Hello, everybody," she cried, blowing kisses to right and left. "Daddy and Chris will be a little bit late. Very big do last night." She rolled her eyes.

Most smiled politely except one young man near Chloe who muttered something very waspish but funny. Though Tara obviously considered herself a young leader of society she wasn't terribly well liked. Something she was oblivious to. Now she made a bee-line for Gabriel, finding an empty space beside him when really there was none.

"Darling, how lovely to see you," she cooed, grasping his arm and kissing his cheek.

Chloe, who wanted no fuss, moved off.

Sir Llew and Christopher Freeman arrived about thirty minutes later and a short time after that their hostess carolled very sweetly, "Luncheon everybody."

"You'll sit with me, won't you?" Christopher, who had all but bolted himself to Chloe's side, now begged. "Come on, pick up a plate," he urged. "There's a simply marvellous vast buffet. Tara's well and truly appropriated your friend, McGuire, if that's who you're looking for."

Which was the case, Chloe was forced to admit, chagrined. She had in fact begun to wonder if they were going to settle themselves perpetually on the upholstered bench of the decking looking out over the view. Tara chatting one hundred to the dozen.

A lot of guests were quaffing champagne and Chardonnay at the rate of knots and Chloe wondered, too, just how they were going to get home. Maybe there were fleets of buses waiting she hadn't seen.

The buffet was indeed marvellous, served on large Indonesian platters filled with whole salmon, smoked salmon, lobsters and prawns, ham, crisp spiced chicken,

with great bowls of salad, pork and beef dishes, cold and
hot, the latter cooked in the Thai fashion and served with
high fluffy piles of rice and stir-fried vegetables.

Although Freeman had wanted Chloe all to himself,
others joined in, filling up the tables, including McGuire
who had managed to lose Tara for a few minutes.

"Where have *you* been?" Chloe asked him a little
coolly when he drew up a chair beside her.

"Surely you haven't missed me?" His black gaze was
mocking.

"This is a party, isn't it?" She turned her face a little
away from him so he couldn't see her expression.

"So why are you down in the doldrums?"

"I am *not!*" Chloe swung her head back, looking at
him closely. His skin had picked up sun. It was glowing
golden. "You're teasing, aren't you?"

"Yes, isn't it too awful? What about you and
Freeman? I've told you not to hurl yourself at him."

"You know perfectly well that's not what I'm doing," Chloe said, responding to his bantering tone.

"Pay no attention to me."

"I won't."

"Ah, there you are, Gabe." Tara returned from the
buffet, her plate piled precariously high. "Chloe, move
over, there's a good girl. I want to sit beside Gabe."

"I was here first." Chloe looked up brightly.

"I guess she was." Gabe fetched up a sigh. "I never
thought I'd see the day when beautiful women would
fight over me."

"Who said anything about fighting? I only want to
stay out of the sun." Chloe adjusted her chair fractionally so she was under one of the white sail awnings.

Tara laughed in annoyance and sat down abruptly, her
expression changing as Christopher Freeman came
charging back to Chloe carrying another bottle of Moët.

"No more for me, thank you, Christopher," Chloe said when he set down a flute in front of her.

"Goodness me, another one won't hurt you," he said in an amused but somewhat impatient tone.

"Another one and someone will have to wake me up. No, two's the limit. Especially in the middle of the day."

"I'd like another, Chris," Tara said, clutching the glass and holding it up to him.

"What about you, Gabe?" Freeman asked after he had satisfied Tara.

"No, thanks. I have to make it down the mountain."

"What a couple of spoilsports you are," Freeman drawled.

"We try to be," McGuire said.

"I've already asked my hostess if I can stay the night." A male guest seated near them flashed a white smile. "This is wonderful food. I don't know what to start on first."

It was much later when Chloe was repairing her makeup in the powder room, Tara dashed in and locked the door.

"Listen, just give it to me straight," she said breathlessly. "Are you after Gabe?"

Chloe scrunched a few of her loose curls before she answered. "Maybe he needs a woman like me in his life."

"*Tell* me." Tara had an odd expression on her face, half pleading, half frenzy.

"If it makes you feel any better, Tara, I'm not after anyone," Chloe said kindly. "I'm not ready to settle down."

"I think you are." Tara clicked her tongue. "This is the *third* time I've seen you with Gabe."

"Do you think I ought to apologise?" Chloe glanced at her watch. She really wanted to go home. The day had been hot and brilliantly fine but they could be in for one of Summer's late afternoon thunderstorms.

"Gabe and I have been getting on just fine," Tara was saying. "We're a lot more than *friends*."

"Oh, yes?" Was it possible?

"I had to take this opportunity to talk to you for a few minutes, Chloe. You mightn't have realised the situation."

"I had heard the gossip."

"Exactly!" Tara burst out triumphantly. "If you know the score you won't try to steal him off me, will you?"

"It's a free country," Chloe joked.

"I'd advise you to listen." Tara's voice slid down to sullen. "I could take measures."

"That's not a very pleasant prospect to contemplate," Chloe said. "Are you going to open the door? I bet there's a long queue out there."

Tara moved backwards, stretching out an arm blindly, trying to unlock the door.

"Just remember, your career is in your own hands," she warned.

CHAPTER FIVE

THEY had a slight argument in the car, Chloe brooding about her run-in with Tara. She didn't know what exactly drove her. It couldn't possibly be defined as *jealousy,* could it?

"Everyone seems to know the true story about you and Tara but me," she said, regarding McGuire's rugged dark face. It looked irritated.

"I don't know if I know it myself, Chloe," he said.

"You keep telling me no romance, but she seemed sincere."

"Where does the girl get it from?" McGuire mocked.

"Why would she warn me off?"

He shrugged. "Well she obviously thinks she could be the woman in my life, lucky girl."

"No *could be* about it. She told me you were much more than friends."

"God, that's an old line," he said in disgust. "Anyway what does it have to do with you, Cavanagh. You're not ready for any big romance."

"Certainly not with *you,* McGuire." Not very complimentary. Not even strictly true.

"Why should I believe you?" he countered. "I've only kissed you twice yet you made every other kiss I've shared pale into insignificance."

Chloe bit her lip. "It was hard *not* to respond," she said, especially when she was driven by unfamiliar passion.

"So there *is* a possibility," he asked, sounding more satirical than serious, "I could approach you on bended knee?"

"We were talking about *Tara*. How's she going to put paid to my career?"

He sobered. "I *told* you, Chloe. She can't do it."

"I don't want to labour this, but I've got one word for her and it's Trouble. You said yourself Sir Llew is trying to promote a match."

"Understandable. Sir Llew wants a strong man to take Tara off his hands. He's worked hard all his life giving her everything she wants."

"And a bit of a handful, is she?" Chloe asked with some point.

"I wouldn't know. What *is* this incredible attack upon me, Cavanagh? My little dalliance with Tara adds up to a big fat nothing. While Freeman is well into the chase?"

Chloe thought for a moment, remembering back. "I did my best to give him no encouragement. At least I hope I did. If you want to know, on closer scrutiny, I really don't like him."

"But you'd rather die than show it?"

"That would have been very bad manners, Gabriel. The party was in his honour."

"And all in all, we enjoyed it. Freeman was very put out when you decided to leave."

"So what? Tara didn't look so happy, either."

"True. Now can we get off these people. It's silly to argue. The house was magnificent, our hosts were delightful, the food was splendid. Now I realise we should have left twenty minutes earlier. I think we're in for a thunderstorm."

Chloe raised her head to peer through the windscreen. "It should be short and sweet. I just hope we make it further down the mountain."

"You're not seriously worried are you?" He glanced at her in concern.

"No, a little on edge. I don't like it when people go out of their way to be unpleasant."

"I don't like it, either, but put it out of your head. There's nothing between Tara and me. I took her out a few times…"

"Kissed her a few times?"

"Fair enough, but I didn't sleep with her, Chloe. Why don't you ask right out?"

"Far better I mind my own business," she said. Otherwise she would confirm his crazy suspicions that she was jealous.

Halfway down the mountain a station wagon suddenly emerged from a hidden driveway a couple of hundred yards in front of them, causing McGuire to brake abruptly while the other vehicle, very slow to move off, picked up speed. A woman was driving. There didn't seem to be anyone else in the car but there was a Baby on Board sticker affixed to the rear window.

"Wouldn't you know it," McGuire grumbled. "An overcautious driver and not a lot of places to overtake her. Surely she'd have done better to wait until we went past?"

"Maybe she didn't even see you, or she's got something against Jaguar drivers."

"We're running the risk of driving into the storm," McGuire said. "It seems to be over the mountain, wouldn't you say?"

Chloe looked out at the darkening sky. The billowing clouds were shaped rather like galleons, the sails pierced with blinding rays of sunlight that soon went out. The rain came down. At first lightly, then in a crashing torrent. McGuire turned his lights on, as did the vehicle ahead.

"At least we're nearly there," he said quietly. "We'll stop at the bottom and take shelter until the worst of it is over. Tropical storms are always short-lived affairs."

"I don't like it, Gabriel," Chloe suddenly said, and relaxed a pent-up breath.

"You're perfectly safe." He didn't turn his head, but spoke reassuringly.

"Not *us*." She shook her head.

"What's the matter, Chloe?" he asked.

"I don't know."

"Tell me what you're thinking. Share it." He could feel an answering energy building up inside himself.

"Someone could have an accident," she said.

"Well, Chloe, God willing, it's not going to be us. I'm a good driver and this is a very safe car."

"I know, Gabriel. I'm just going on instinct." She was, she realised, keeping her eyes trained on the vehicle that had now disappeared around the bend.

"You think it might be the station wagon?" he asked in surprise. "She's driving too cautiously to come to much harm. She's a nervous driver in fact." It was just as he said it, McGuire felt his first frisson of alarm.

As they rounded the steep curve both of them expecting to see the station wagon ahead, they were confounded by an empty road. There was no station wagon. No other vehicle.

"Where did she go?" Chloe was feeling so alarmed she was finding it difficult to swallow.

There were no farm houses, no dwellings on this stretch of the road. Nothing. Only as they drove slowly further on, they could see through a break in the tropical shrubbery a dry creek bed that was rapidly filling with water. About thirty feet along the creek bed was the station wagon lying on its hood.

"My God!" McGuire responded immediately, finding a safe place to stop. "She's gone over the side. We couldn't see any skid marks for the rain."

"And just look at the water!" Chloe cried. "I can't

see her moving about. Gabriel, we've got to get down there."

"Get on the car phone. Get help," he said, opening out his door. "Leave this to me, Chloe. It could be dangerous."

The sound of the rain was deafening. No wonder they hadn't heard anything. While McGuire picked his way down the ragged slope to the creek bed, Chloe dialled the 000 emergency number, proceeding to give all the relevant information; the exact location of the accident, the make of the vehicle, and the fact there appeared to be only one occupant, a woman driver. How marvellous these mobile phones were in an emergency, she thought. One shouldn't be without one. She threw open the passenger door and stepped out onto the slippery verge. It was still pouring and she saw to her horror the creek bed all but dry thirty minutes before, was now a raging torrent with debris in the form of fallen branches and twigs, being carried down from further upstream. Chloe had seen a flash flood before today. She knew exactly how bad things could get. She had to get to Gabriel. Lend him her assistance. She wasn't afraid of the water, though she realised she could be swept off her feet. She was an excellent swimmer.

Gabriel, meanwhile, was working his legs hard against the force of the water. Beside the car he now saw there was a baby in the rear car seat flailing and wriggling, its small face red with fright and rage, but mercifully held by the car seat's restraint. The mother appeared to be unconscious, slumped upside down but still strapped in. The next thing he knew, Chloe was sliding down the slope and into the water, working furiously to get to him. He had never seen anyone move so fast.

"There's a baby in here, Chloe," he yelled. "If you can get to her, I'll try to get the mother out."

Help might be coming, but it could be too late.

By now both of them were soaked, a fine spray of rainwater sheening their faces. Gabriel got the rear door open. Chloe fought to reach in, got a hold on the baby with one arm and struggled to release the restraint. She didn't have time to look about for Gabriel who was now on the other side of the car trying his hardest to figure out the best way to release the woman who was noticeably pregnant. He was pretty sure he could grab her, but unconscious, she would be a dead weight. It was at times like this he was thankful he was a big man in his prime, blessed with splendid health and strength. He was going to need it.

"Chloe, get out of here," he shouted as he saw her with the screaming baby cradled in her arms. The mother was bleeding slightly and had a fair bit of swelling on one side of her head.

Chloe tried to oblige. She stood perfectly still for a moment and stared at the rushing water. It would be terrible if she lost her footing. She could even lose her hold on the baby.

"Come on, we're almost there," a voice said in her ear.

I'm some sort of case, Chloe thought. I'll just have to get used to it.

"To the right," the voice urged gently.

Chloe didn't hesitate though she was nearly up to her waist in swirling water. The rain was still coming down but the storm was losing its violence. Chloe proceeded with caution, planting one foot after the other, weighing down her body in between. At one stage it crossed Chloe's mind someone was leading her. Once she staggered as her foot hit a hidden rock, only to have herself righted.

"Don't be so hasty," the voice gently admonished.

"No," she replied, instantly obedient.

Finally she waded out and sat down hard on the bank,

realising the baby had stopped its wailing and was staring with great interest at a point past her shoulder, but she didn't turn to look.

"Gabriel, are you still there?" she shouted in a desperate panic. The station wagon had shifted position in the surging waters, the rear end swinging towards her. "Gabriel!" she cried, her voice full of anxiety.

"He's safe," the voice said.

"Who *are* you?" Chloe whispered, feeling a wonderful rush of comfort. No one answered. How could they?

A moment more and Gabriel loomed into sight, a colossus to Chloe's eyes, carrying the woman in his strong arms. At one point he stumbled and Chloe's stomach gave a sick somersault, but then he jerked upright as though someone had helped him find his balance.

"My hero," Chloe cried emotionally when he was almost at the bank. "How are you?"

"Hurting a bit." He was huffed.

"Stay with it," she urged him with great intensity. "You deserve a citation." And a great big kiss, as well.

The rain stopped abruptly, turned off like a tap. To mark the storm's passing a beautiful rainbow, "the bride of the rain," spread its magic arc across the sky, rose, violet, yellow and green.

Chloe began to jiggle the baby, filled with such tremendous relief she was alight. "Don't be afraid, darling," she crooned. Mummy was safe lying on the bank, dazed but conscious. Chloe snuggled the little creature close, immensely grateful it was summer, for although they were both wet, neither of them was cold. In fact, their clothing was drying remarkably quickly.

Gabriel turned away from his patient for one fraught moment to catch Chloe's face to him. He wanted to kiss her madly, triumphantly. And he did, putting his heart and soul into it, taking her sweet mouth with passionate urgency.

They heard the siren before an ambulance came into sight, followed by a police car. Both vehicles parked up on the verge and in another few minutes people were surging down the slope.

"Thank God," Chloe murmured, and the breeze whispered, Amen.

They waited until the ambulance left with mother and child, and the police said they could go home. A tow truck had already arrived and preparations were under way to right the vehicle before winching it out of the creek. The bed of the creek had been baked so hard the water was still rushing freely, holding its level, unable to soak into the soil. It was hampering operations but Chloe and Gabriel were happy to leave it to the experts. The police weren't happy about the "balding" condition of the station wagon's front tyres, the probable cause of the accident.

The woman had a concussion, her blood pressure was up, but she was quite coherent and anxious to thank Gabriel and Chloe for coming to their rescue and almost certainly averting a tragedy. Other motorists coming down the mountain afterward might have responded to their plight but by then mother and child could have drowned.

"We intend to call attention to this fine piece of rescue work," the policeman in charge told them.

"We don't want any publicity." Chloe shook her head. "We just did what anyone else would do."

"Perhaps, but I assure you not so well." There was an undertone of amazement in the policeman's voice. "I can understand your friend here performing such a feat, big strong bloke, but for you to ford a flash flood and rescue the baby gets to be a bit mind-boggling. You want to take out a lottery ticket."

The ambulance officer who had draped them both in blankets, seemed genuinely amazed when they returned them because their clothes were almost dry.

"Even with the heat of the sun, I would have thought it would take a lot longer than that," he said.

Chloe fingertipped her lawn shirt. The texture was as smooth as if it had been steam pressed, with no trace of the dirt and grit that muddied the swollen creek. Gabriel's clothes were the same.

They were very quiet on the journey back to Chloe's house, both shaken and trying to get the events of the afternoon straight in their minds.

"How did you do it, Chloe?" McGuire finally asked.

"Don't ask," she murmured helplessly. "I don't think we're supposed to ask."

"What does *that* mean?" He shot a glance at her. Her hair had dried into a glorious mass of waves and ringlets haloing her face. He adored it.

"Don't you get the feeling it was some kind of mystical experience, dear, strong Gabriel?"

McGuire watched a flight of brilliantly coloured lorikeets swoop above the car. "It's been ages since I had a mystical experience, Chloe, but you could be right."

"Have you *ever* had one?" Chloe asked, intensely interested in the answer. Gabriel, she had learned, was a very deep and unusual person.

"Once when I was a child." The dark cloud settled down over his face again.

"You don't want to tell me," she said gently, aware of the pain in him.

"It wasn't a good experience, Chloe, but if I tell you, I can't play it down."

Chloe leaned over, put out her hand and softly touched his cheek. "Was it about your father?"

"I'd done something," he began quietly, reflectively. "I'm not saying I wasn't a wild kid. I was. It was the price of growing up in a violent home. Dad took a belt to me and couldn't seem to stop. I was only about ten and I thought maybe I was going to die. Anyway, in my helplessness, hopelessness, I called out to my guardian angel to help me. I remember it very clearly. I said. 'If you're there, now's the time to help me.' I don't know what happened next. *I* saw nothing but Dad sure did. He dropped the belt and bolted up the cellar stairs as though the devil himself was after him. Fortunately for me, it wasn't the devil. I still have the unshakeable belief my guardian angel manifested himself in some way. My father didn't touch me for a long time after and never again so badly. Whatever he saw, it really shook him up."

"And you've had to live with the pain of it all."

"There were odd moments of happiness. In the right mood when things came together, Dad became the person my mother married. No ugliness, no menace. He was an entirely different human being."

"Did he never have counselling?" Chloe asked.

"No, he never sought help. He thought he was *beyond* help. It's the end, really, when we give in to despair."

Chloe was beginning to see what it must have been like for the young Gabriel to pull himself out of such a tragic environment. Like today, he had shown great courage.

When they arrived home a BTQ8 van was parked outside the house.

"Oh, no!" Chloe said in dismay. "They've got the story."

"See what it's like when the spotlight's turned on you?" McGuire said laconically.

"I don't want to do this, Gabriel."

"And you think I do? I hate to have my picture taken let alone being presented as some sort of hero. Come on, let's face it. It's news. People like to see this sort of thing.''

As they drove in the gates, the van followed them, everyone alighting at pretty well the same time.

"Hi, there!" Jennifer Bourne walked towards them, an attractive figure in a smart red suit with gold buttons. "Had a nice time up the mountain?"

"We enjoyed ourselves. You've got the story, right?" McGuire said wryly.

"Sure we have, Gabe. At least half a dozen people phoned us. After we finish here, we're off to the hospital to have a few words with mother and babe.''

"The baby won't be giving much away," Gabe said dryly. "He's all of eight months old."

"You know what I mean, Boss." Jennifer shrugged. "Why so shy? I would have thought you'd love to get your picture in the paper. They'll turn up, of course. Maggie in publicity wants it, plus a spot on the news.''

"Let's get it over," was all McGuire said.

"Aren't you going to invite us in, Chloe?" Jennifer tried to smile at her limelight-stealing colleague, but didn't quite succeed.

"Sure," Chloe said, realising they didn't stand a chance.

"So when did you get to change your clothes?" Jennifer asked, her eyes raking Chloe's petite figure.

Chloe, poised at the top of the steps, turned back. "We haven't."

"I find that very hard to believe," Jennifer drawled.

"Do you want to keep it a little secret?"

"No secret," McGuire said in a no-nonsense voice. "These are the same clothes we wore to the party. They've dried off in the heat.''

Jennifer, faced with their immaculate appearances, couldn't help herself. "Did you find a motel?"

"I beg your pardon," McGuire turned on her, frowning.

"Just joking, Gabe." Jennifer backed off hastily. "The two of you look like you've just stepped out of a fashion magazine. Weren't you supposed to be waist-deep in water?"

"What the hell do you think? That's why you're here."

Jennifer didn't look any too convinced but she had trouble fitting her scenario to the time frame.

It took roughly forty minutes before it was all over and afterwards McGuire stood up to take his leave.

"I'll leave you in peace, Chloe."

It was way too early for him to go. Chloe didn't think she could accept being on her own, although Christopher Freeman had at one point during the lunch suggested that they might like to go out to see "The Phantom of the Opera" with supper afterwards. As a suggestion it had had no appeal whatsoever and she had turned him down. Chloe wasn't attracted to Freeman in any capacity and she didn't fancy being anyone's Number Four wife, if indeed such was the intention. McGuire, with whom she had shared a somewhat jangled relationship and always on the work level, was now causing her heartache. For one thing, she had been too quick to judge him. *Prejudge* him really. And she'd been mistaken. He certainly was abrasive at times, very demanding as the station boss, but he was by no means the diamond in the rough she had sought to label him. He had many, many facets and considerable brilliance. She confessed to herself now her strong resistance to him had been emotional. It was as he said. She really did fear a close bond. Love was everything in life. The loss of it was appalling, involving lots of grief and pain. She should know.

"Chloe?" McGuire looked down at her slumped a little forlornly in an armchair.

"Oh, I'm sorry, Gabriel." Quickly she raised her head. "I'm feeling the reaction, I suppose."

"Is there anything at all I can get you?" he asked, concern in his dark eyes.

"No, I'm fine." She stood up, fixing a bright smile on her face. "Do you suppose we'll make the six o'clock news?"

"That's what they're aiming for."

She was about to say, "Do you want to stay to watch it?" but he seemed anxious to go. Perhaps he'd had enough of her and the misadventures that seemed to follow her.

It was Freeman, in fact, who rang later in the evening, sounding a little hung over and clearly surprised to find her at home.

"I thought I'd ring on the off chance you were still there," he explained. It was eight o'clock. "I thought you said you had a previous engagement."

"Which I had to cry off, Christopher," Chloe lied. She was facing the mirror above the console in the hallway, now she made a face at herself. "I've developed a splitting headache."

"No wonder, darling," he said with superficial sympathy. "You've been on television, do you know that? You and Gabe."

"I did see it." Chloe made a real effort not to sound so formal. On the one hand she didn't want to offend Christopher Freeman and put him off the interview, on the other she didn't want to give him the slightest encouragement to pursue her. Whether for some transient pleasure or a more serious involvement. Obviously he took their big age difference lightly. He kept on chatting at great length so Chloe had to pull up a chair, but finally he rang off, telling her she was wonderful and he couldn't wait for their interview and afterwards take her out to dinner.

Once off the phone Chloe looked around the silent house. Loneliness was almost tangible. Why hadn't Gabriel rung? It really was terribly laid back of him or maybe he was too busy dressing to go out again. She wasn't sure of anything he did. There could very well be an assortment of women in his life. All the women who worked with her found him outrageously sexy. She had even accepted his heart-thudding excitement. And he was a wonderful kisser. She might be a traumatised virgin but she had had plenty of kisses in her time. All of them totally eclipsed by McGuire's expertise and sexual intensity.

She could get into terrible trouble falling in love with someone like Gabriel McGuire. She wasn't prepared, either, for the fact his not ringing hurt her so much. Chloe walked nearer the hall mirror. Stared at herself. What she saw was a wistful young woman with good creamy skin, a mop of wild red-gold hair, she had washed it, rather unhappy blue eyes, the colour intensified by the colour of the satin flower-and-bird embroidered kimono she had bought while on a short assignment in Japan. It was such a lovely thing. It had immediately caught her eye. These days the catwalks were full of models wearing underwear in the guise of evening wear. She could go anywhere in this if she had to, only there wasn't anywhere to go. She could ring one of her friends, of course. Sally was always good for a laugh. Beth was a lovely person, hopelessly shy, but good for comfort.

No, something was ailing her. Something she didn't want to give a name.

Chloe found herself a book, a new paperback, and settled down on the sofa. A compelling psychological thriller, she read on the jacket. She had to read the first few pages a couple of times over to make sense of it. Too many characters, she decided. It needed too much of her concentration. As usual when she was very much alone, Chloe's thoughts turned with great melancholy to her mother. In the early days she had pleaded to bring her mother home; to look after her. She could pay for a carer when she was at work. She could work her legs off. Which she had, but the doctors had convinced her her mother was much better off in the nursing home where she could receive around-the-clock professional care.

Chloe let her head fall back against the sofa, the tears coming into her eyes. Now and again she indulged herself in the luxury of grief, when mostly she had to keep over the top of it to survive. But never to talk to her mother again? Never to hear her voice? Never to laugh together, as they had in the halcyon days. They'd had such fun. Never to exchange little presents. They had done that all the time, delighting in surprising one another with small gifts. The tears flowed down Chloe's cheeks, as deadly misery flowed over her.

"Don't give in to despair, Chloe," the unseen voice said. "Don't give up on prayer." Little multicoloured lights like tiny stars shone before Chloe's eyes. Some extraordinary refraction of light through her tears. Chloe sat up abruptly and went to find tissues to dry her eyes. All she ever got from these sessions was a blinding headache.

It was when she was in her bedroom the front doorbell rang. For an instant she stood transfixed then moved to the curtains, peering out.

Gabriel.

Propelled by a force totally out of her control, she ran, throwing open the door and staring up into his increasingly familiar face.

"Chloe, I was worried about you." His dark, brooding gaze moved intensely over her, seeing the unhappiness and the tears that still beaded her long eyelashes, making them stick together.

"Why didn't you ring?" she accused him. "Didn't you want to talk to me?"

"Why?" He gave a jangled laugh. "Chloe, I'm desperate to find the right words."

"You didn't want to share it with me? To say it was a moving little segment?"

"Chloe." He moved his hands a little helplessly.

"I'm glad you came back," she said in a breathless, out-of-control voice. "I want you to stay."

"Dear God!" He took the door from her nerveless hands, shut it behind them, grasping a handful of her hair and pulling her into his arms. "What is it? What's wrong?"

"I'm aching." Her voice was muffled up against his chest. "Sometimes I think I can't take it."

"I'm here now." It was wonderful to enfold her in his arms, to feel her slight beautiful body curving into his. Wonderful to give comfort. Only she started to stir, to move against him. He could feel the heat grow in him, the molten rush of blood through his veins. Was it just an aching child he held? A young person who had virtually lost both her parents in tragic circumstances? It was a woman's body she possessed. He could feel the softness of her breasts crushed against him, the shape of her beneath the too thin covering of her robe. One part of him, the excited male, wanted to tear it off her, but she was totally vulnerable and deep inside him he abhorred violence in any form.

"You're so beautiful," he said. "So very, very beautiful."

She lifted her head, startling him with the expression in her eyes. It couldn't be naked hunger, a hunger to match his own?

Then he was kissing her, not as tenderly as he intended but desperately, passionately, scarcely letting her breathe.

Stop, he thought. Don't frighten her. He wrenched his mouth way, cradling her, kissing her hair and her cheeks and her small, perfect chin. Not alarming her seemed very important, yet no man could be expected to endure such temptation. He forced himself to some kind of calm though his whole body was racked with the most exquisite pain.

"Gabriel, make love to me," she whispered. A plea, no doubt at all, and it tugged at his heart.

"Chloe, I *can't*." How in God's name had he said that?

"I need loving so badly."

Not *his* loving.

"Chloe, I can't do this." He held her firmly by the shoulders, half pressure, half bringing her back to control.

Her lovely face was tragic. "When you said you *wanted* me? You didn't even mean it."

"It's more than my life's worth to hurt you," he replied simply.

"Gabriel, I'm not a doll. I won't break."

"You're not sure of what you're doing, either. You don't love me."

She flushed with something approaching shame, pain, regret.

"Gabriel, I can't. Don't ask me. When I'm stronger, if Mum ever gets better, I'll make a huge effort, I promise. But for now I want you to love me physically. I don't know *why* when you're the most emotional man I've ever met. But you're good and kind. I just never knew it."

"Shut up," he said with dark, burning eyes. "I'm trying to think what I can come up with. You *are* a virgin, aren't you, Chloe?"

She felt horribly near to tears again. "Does it matter?"

"It matters a great deal," he said with a deep sigh.

"I know there aren't an awful lot of virgins my age about, but yes, I am." Chloe spoke with a false flippancy.

"You must have had a tough time fending off your admirers." He, too, tried unsuccessfully to lighten the tension. But it was quite, quite impossible. "Suppose I just start off kissing you?"

Chloe looked around wildly. "This isn't a joke, McGuire."

"No." There was a rather grim smile on his face. "The truth of it is, Chloe, I don't trust myself to make love to you. You've always seemed so incredibly delicate to me. Hell, the very first day I met you you made me feel overpowering. And hideous."

She was shocked. "When all I thought was you were rather tall and imposing with very beautiful dark brown eyes. I know my behaviour was hurtful, Gabriel, and I'm sorry."

"How sorry?" he asked, those dark eyes probing her face.

"Why should you be *sensitive?*" she asked helplessly.

"Only to you. You could fall in love with me, Chloe, if only you let yourself."

"When you're making such a fuss about making love to me?" she retorted.

"That's hardly surprising. I've made love to lots of pretty girls in my time but you're something else again."

"You mean, a virgin?" she said sadly.

"No, it's not that. Not entirely. In other ways you're pretty sophisticated. You're far from shy. You're very good at what you do, but I don't want to alienate you with my rough male desires. I have a feeling it's too new to you."

Chloe's eyes began to blaze. "Is it possible, I suppose it's just possible, you're trying to get square with me?

You want to teach me a lesson? Given the things I've said, it's understandable.''

He felt crammed up to the neck with talk. It wasn't talk he wanted. Neither did she. He lifted her in his arms with great ease, carrying her into the living room and settling her across his knees on the nearest sofa.

"The minute you say *stop,* God help me, I promise I will, even if I can't bear the pain.''

"You're really weird, McGuire,'' she said with a wobbling little laugh.

"How weird?''

"Tara, for instance, wouldn't put up with this. She'd demand to be satisfied.''

"I can't pretend she wouldn't,'' he said dryly.

"Then you have....'' She never got any further. He twined his hand through her long thick hair so she couldn't turn her head away, then began kissing her, his mouth very gentle at first, the tip of his tongue curling around hers.

Such a soft beginning yet the build-up of excitement was so extreme it soared.

"Well, Chloe?'' He lifted his mouth fractionally when she moaned.

"No... I mean yes.'' She was seething with need and filled with a wild impatience for him to kiss her again. She feared, really feared, he would stop, so she raised her body, letting her finger trace the deep indentation in his chin.

"Chloe,'' he muttered, the depth of his desire glittering out of his eyes.

"Let *me* kiss *you.*'' She pushed his head back, climbing a little on him so she could cover his mouth.

He couldn't seem to stand it. Groaning softly, almost in anguish. The thought made her kiss him again. There was so much tension in his powerfully built body. She could feel the muscles of his face tightening under her hands.

"What are you trying to do to me, Chloe?" His voice was low and deep.

"I'm thanking you for saving that woman's life." She wanted to curl herself around him like a cat.

He took her light, fine-boned hands in his. "I've had quite enough thanks for that." He knew she wasn't aware of the powerful unconscious seductiveness in her, this vivid, fiercely hurting creature.

"I'm sorry, Gabriel." Chloe didn't meet his eyes.

"What for?" he asked gently.

"It must seem mad to you the way I'm acting."

"You're desperate for comfort, Chloe." He stroked her hair. "I only wish there was something more attached to it."

"My problems aren't your problems, either."

"I want you to share them, Chloe. You've had to live with too high a level of anxiety and grief. There's nothing more in this world I want than to make love to you." Dear God, how much. "Only something—someone— seems to be telling me I'd be taking advantage of you past a certain point."

"So what is this point, Gabriel?" she asked in a strange little voice.

"Well, I'm allowed to kiss you," he said, and began again. From wounded, Chloe became soothed. From over-excited she found absolute delight, as she discovered just how miraculous kissing could be. There was some kind of magic in him that gave her strength. His kisses deepened then lightened at just the right moment so she was able to surface from the tumult of emotions. His touch was tender but elusive on her body, constantly skimming but not stopping as though the consequences would be fatal in some way. Yet every part of her he touched, he changed. The lightest caress penetrated not only her body but her soul. It was a stunning piece of lovemaking, an exercise in healing, so that after a while Chloe began to feel she was flying. There were even wings attached to her shoulderblades. He would *have* to know she couldn't resist him.

I've got to have her, Gabriel thought. I've got to have and hold this beautiful creature. But his iron determination to give her time, to give her space, was rapidly leaving him, vanishing like a morning mist. He longed to cup her small naked breasts. He had never seen anything so pretty in his life as the sight of them through the drooping neckline of her feather-light nightgown. He was holding her high up against his heart but he longed to pick her up and carry her through to her bedroom, make love to her at will, make her his whether she loved him or not. His own emotions were bubbling out of control. He'd had to summon all his strength to keep at this level but he was becoming madly elated, wild for more. God help him, he wasn't made of stone. He bent over Chloe very carefully, her eyes were shut but her face was so radiant it brought a lump to his throat. He hadn't truly recognised his feelings for her until that moment. Oh, he had always known how much he *wanted* her. What he hadn't properly realised was, he loved her with all his heart. She was the object of his greatest hopes and desires.

"Chloe!"

If she opened her eyes and smiled at him with her lovely sweet smile he would carry her away, lay her back on her bed, peel the clothes from her. He could feel the trembling right through his body. The white heat of desire....

It was the rush of wind through the house that did it. The long filmy curtains began to dance and the lustres on the chandeliers began to sway and tinkle, playing a stream of silver music. A little ornament went over but didn't break.

"What was that?" Chloe sat up, literally snapping out of her dream state.

Gabriel laughed wryly. "I told you someone else was calling the shots."

"What do you mean?" Chloe sprang to her feet, going to the French doors where the curtains were billowing and swinging from side to side as though in the grip of a stiff breeze. "That's funny," she said, staring out into the night. "There doesn't seem to be any wind out there. The palm trees are quite still."

Gabriel stood up, righting the piece of Meissen depicting two winged cherubs holding a cradle in the shape of a swan. It was a lovely piece, mercifully quite intact. He nursed it for a moment—no expert—but realising it was valuable. "What about a cup of coffee?" he suggested as though he was only too willing to cooperate with the unexplainable. "Personally I'm thinking of joining a paranormal society."

Chloe, busy clamping the flying curtains, dropped them as she became aware they simply weren't blowing anymore. Like Gabriel, she had the decidedly odd feeling they were in the hands of some irresistible force.

"What a good idea," she agreed a little shakily, struck by the dazzle of the twin chandeliers. She looked towards Gabriel, wondering at his transformation from adversary and sparring partner to lover. The speed with which it had happened took her breath away. She stared at him for quite a while, giving each one of his features her startled attention. She felt as though she had never truly seen him before. She felt exquisitely shy of him, as well, yet deeply *connected*. She felt she would most likely die if he suddenly went away and left her.

"Chloe?" he prompted gently, thinking he would al-

ways hold the sight of her at that moment in his heart.
He held out his hand to her.

There was a huge difference in the way they were
saying each other's names, Chloe thought. Formerly it
had seemed like throwaway banter, cheeky, cheerful,
sardonic, outright taunting. Now there was a beautiful
unusual *significance* that became more apparent each
time they spoke one another's name.

"I'll always remember this night, Gabriel," she said,
walking towards him as though drawn by a powerful,
shining magnet.

Another severe test of my resolution, Gabe thought,
his heart thudding, but he didn't want to push his luck.
The moment when he could make his beautiful Chloe
his own was close by but not yet. Still he allowed his
eyes to reveal the depths of his feelings. "Walk me to
the door, my little Chloe," he said. "I wish I could stay
forever but I think I've been told to go."

CHAPTER SIX

IT WASN'T yet dawn. The nursing home was quiet, yet outside Delia's window a bird sang as though enchanted, the sweetness and purity of its tone causing sparkling tears like dewdrops to spring into her eyes.

Tears? She somehow felt she hadn't wept for a long time.

Delia lay absolutely still in the dark room, trying to concentrate on where she was. She was concentrating with all of her being, aware some extraordinary energy was oscillating around her body, scanning her heart, her muscles, her skin, exploring the control systems of the body that for so long had been under attack. She didn't want to draw a breath unless this mysterious source of energy ceased its operations. Now she felt it was scanning her brain, locking into the complex network of nerve connections that sent down instructions for her body to act on.

Regaining mental clarity, Delia was still only half aware of what was happening to her. But she knew to keep perfectly *still*. Being still was part of it, allowing the mysterious force to continue its work.

Time passed. Perhaps an hour. She didn't know. It was still dark, but she felt totally at peace, able to comprehend that something monumental was happening to her, that her flawed brain and body were communing with a great power. An infinite power. A power for good.

Delia closed her eyes tightly so she could pay closer attention to what was happening inside her. Aware the whole time the night-bird was continuing to pour out its heart in rapture.

132

Delia's brain was beginning to fire in a normal pattern. Lying there with her eyes closed she realised she wasn't in her own home. She was in some sort of hospital. She wondered where Chloe was. Chloe, her beloved girl. She couldn't trust herself to think of Peter, her husband. Had Peter gone? And Timothy, her baby boy. The child who had died. So cruel, so cruel. She had adored him from the moment they had put him into her arms.

Timothy Michael Cavanagh. Michael after her father. Both of her children had inherited her colouring, the distinctive red-gold hair and bright blue eyes.

Tim!

Very warily, Delia opened her eyes.

"Timmy, what in the world are you doing there?" she cried in the greatest amazement.

Although it was still dark outside, there was a shaft of light in the room. Such a vision! Like being locked inside a lovely great crystal.

Only Tim, who now approached the bed to stand beside her, wasn't eighteen months old. He was, she thought dazedly, more like eight.

"Darling boy, have I been asleep all this time?" she asked, full of wonder.

Tim bent, breathed gently on her, kissed her cheek.

It was perfect. A kiss straight from Heaven filling her heart with light.

Her window was in direct view. A ray of light was beaming through it with the beauty and radiance of distilled moonlight.

When Delia looked again for Tim he wasn't there.

"Timmy?" He couldn't go away. She had missed him so terribly all these years.

Where had he gone? She had heard no door opening. Where had the time gone? The years? She was certain it was Tim. Now it seemed impossible. Delia lifted her hands as her brain gave the message to her motor system to her muscles. There was still the soft glow in the room so she could see her hands clearly. They were very thin but still pretty. Peter had always said she had the prettiest hands in the world.

Peter.

The name struck like a knife in her heart, only when she turned her head Peter and Timothy were standing by the bed, hand in hand, their eyes shining with love for her, their bodies illumined as if starlight was glowing through them. How could she doubt it when they were smiling at her so lovingly? Her weak body was feeling so much stronger. *Stronger.* She felt like she could get up out of bed. Go to them. They held out their hands.

At six o'clock that morning when the nursing home was abustle with the start of a new day, Marge Harding, Delia's most devoted nurse, came into her room, wearing her usual bright smile. No matter Mrs. Cavanagh never responded. She was a lovely lady. It was Marge's earnest prayer one day she might be rid of her tragic disorder, or taken quietly in her sleep. Only Delia wasn't in the bed. To Marge's horror, her patient was lying curled up on the floor. Marge bent over her in alarm. Her first thought was Delia had died, only as she reached for Delia's wrist she found a pulse.

"Mrs. Cavanagh, Mrs. Cavanagh," she cried out in distress. She knew well enough the pulse rate was within normal limits, something very strange was happening here.

Another nurse, Marge's friend, Nora, hurried in, alerted by Marge's loud, anxious cry. She swooped on them and as she did so, Delia opened her blue eyes.

"Good morning, Nurse." Delia smiled as though she hadn't been "away" for a single minute. "Good morning to both of you. I had the most extraordinary dream last night." Unassisted she sat up, staring into their rapt faces. "I dreamed my beloved family came back to me. They *touched* me. My heart, and my soul. They made me strong again for Chloe. My Chloe needs me. I must speak to her."

Both nurses were too stunned to reply, although they were destined to relate the first moments of Mrs. Cavanagh's extraordinary recovery over and over.

There had to be hope to life, Marge thought. Miracles, too.

With God all things are possible.

Chloe received the news within ten minutes of her mother's "awakening," summoned to the nursing home by the matron in charge. Matron sounded thrilled beyond words yet Chloe detected a faint undertone of caution as though this caring professional doubted the evidence of her own eyes.

Chloe who had been sleeping soundly, jumped out of bed as though someone had set fire to it, racing into the bathroom calling aloud, "Oh, my God, Oh, my God!" This was a miracle beyond her imaginings. An answer to her endless prayers. Yet there was an element of terror in it, in case something went wrong. Maybe her mother had only responded for a short time.

"No, I can't think that!" she cried to the bathroom mirror, brushing her teeth and washing her face, splashing water everywhere in her haste.

In her bedroom, she threw herself into the first thing that came to hand, a mulberry T-shirt and jeans. She was so excited she had developed palpitations. Since the day her mother had smiled, over a week before, Chloe hadn't allowed herself to get up her hopes. She had until that day almost been emptied out of hope, but then a candle had flared in her heart, pooling into light and never going out.

She *had* to tell Gabriel. She had to share her consummate joy, Gabriel had become so close to her. He had

seen her mother's smile. He had held her mother's hand
and told her stories much the same as Chloe did herself.
Her tyrannical McGuire was really a man of great
strength and kindness.

It was early. Not yet 6:30 but she was certain Gabriel
wouldn't mind an early morning call. He was probably
used to them. Chloe dialled the number, so filled with
bubbling emotion her hand was shaking. The phone rang
a few times. Perhaps Gabriel was already up making
breakfast. Then the receiver was lifted and a young
woman's lilting voice said very brightly, "Hi, can I help
you?"

For a minute Chloe was flooded with shock. Wrong
number? No, she'd keyed in the correct number.

"Hello," the attractive voice repeated with an upward
inflection.

Chloe, the brilliant young interviewer and outgoing
TV personality, stood trapped, her heart cleft in two.
Mixed in with the shock was a terrible sense of dishon-
ourment, she would have to deal with at some other time.
Not now. Now was for her mother.

She was about to hang up when Gabriel came on,
sounding very brisk and businesslike.

"Who is this?" he demanded.

Chloe tried unsuccessfully to speak.

Gabriel lived alone. His mother lived in Tasmania. He
had no sister. His only female cousin was married and
living in the South Island of New Zealand.

For some reason, no doubt guilt, he suddenly queried
harshly, "Chloe?"

Chloe dropped the phone like a hot coal. Another time
she would have told him what she thought. That there
was absolutely no meaning to the strong bond that was
being forged between them. That she was violently and
deeply shocked. But her mother was waiting for her. Her
mother was her entire life. What was a little heartbreak

compared to having her mother back again? She'd had plenty of hard knocks in life. She could take another one. But beneath the courage she was *stupefied,* heart and brain swelling with tremendous emotion, gratitude, wonder, alongside pain and confusion. Which showed how deeply Gabriel McGuire had penetrated her life.

The phone rang almost immediately after but Chloe ignored it.

Her hands clenched on the wheel to hide their trembling, she drove to the nursing home, stopping momentarily at reception to check it was all right, then racing down the corridors until she came to her mother's room.

She had to pause to catch her breath.

Her mother was sitting in the armchair Chloe normally sat in, dressed in a pretty pink tracksuit someone must have found her, because it was unfamiliar to Chloe. But the glorious smile her mother gave her wasn't.

Her mother was truly back. She was cured. Chloe had no doubts at all. She flew across the room arms outstretched and her mother stood so they came together, of a height, their arms wrapped around one another, each trying to rain the most kisses on the other's face.

"My darling, my darling!" Delia's voice was so filled with love it rang out like a happy bell.

"You've come back." Chloe stared into her mother's sweet face, saw the light in her eyes, the harmony, the serenity, the fire of intelligence. Her soul.

"For you, my little love." Delia clasped her daughter's hand in an ecstasy of togetherness.

Neither was aware of it but the tears of joy were pouring down their faces, spilling like beads of crystal from the fanned edges of their long eyelashes.

Delia pulled Chloe down into an armchair, took the chair opposite, eager to tell her daughter what she could tell no other. "Tim's been here. And your father," she said. "I saw them as plainly as I'm seeing you."

The shared confidence and the look in her mother's eyes had a galvanising effect on Chloe. For a moment her ears buzzed with a cadenza of sound and her heart momentarily shook. Was her mother's miraculous recovery a *total* reality or in some way had she been altered forever?

"No, don't be frightened, my Chloe," Delia begged, seeing the flash of sorry rue and astonishment in her daughter's face. "It is as I'm telling you. I *saw* them. It was no hallucination, so dry your tears, my darling. There's a lot more in store for both of us. Much happiness. It's been given to me to know."

Listening to her mother, Chloe was both enchanted and frightened. Heaven *had* smiled on them surely? So why did she have such difficulty accepting her mother's dream? For *dream* it had to be. Dream so vivid it lived.

While the two women sat in their closeness, Matron, her face rosy with pride and satisfaction in their patient's victory over a very great trauma, showed in Doctor William Gough, a leading neurologist, and the nursing home's senior resident psychiatrist, Doctor Simon Blakely. The great news had gone out. Now the testing would begin. The medical profession found it difficult to accept miracles.

Chloe remained while all the happy preliminaries went on, then as the questions grew more comprehensive, more searching, both men intimated they would like to speak to Delia alone. Both of them had attended her mother for months now. Both of them highly dedicated, kind men.

Chloe left the room, walking some distance along the corridor and taking a seat in an empty waiting room. One of the young nurses brought tea and biscuits to her and she sipped at the tea gratefully. Her head was awhirl.

She feared what her mother might say under questioning. The doctors might look askance on mystical experiences.

There was a slight commotion at the end of the corridor near reception. Curious, Chloe walked to the door of the waiting room and looked out.

Gabriel, dressed as casually as she was, was hurrying down the passageway, heading right for her. A nurse was coming after him, gasping.

"Sir, sir!"

"It's all right," Chloe called to the same nurse who had admitted her, a nurse she knew well. "I know this person."

She couldn't say, "He's a friend." She didn't know *what* to say.

"Chloe." Gabriel closed on her, so tall, so dark, so powerfully built she reverted to feeling overwhelmed. "I rang the house. You didn't answer. I felt desperately worried, then it occurred to me you might be with your mother." Really, it hadn't just occurred to him the idea had been planted like a seed. "Is she all right?"

Chloe tried to respond calmly. "She's regained consciousness. She's talking. She's told me so much. Some of it with the radiance of a vision. Her doctors are with her now." Probably deciding she's a little crazy, Chloe thought, turning her face away abruptly.

"Was it you who rang me this morning?" Gabriel put his hand beneath her chin and turned her face back to him, shaken by the deep withdrawal he sensed in her.

"No."

"I think it was, Chloe," he insisted, his rugged face a little grim.

"A mistake. For both of us."

"Chloe, what are you talking about?" His fine dark eyes were fixed unwaveringly on hers.

"It's all right, you know, Gabriel," she said evasively.

"Sweetheart. Was it because a woman answered the phone?"

She couldn't risk showing her heart, yet she wanted to fling herself at him so their bodies could do the talking. "Well I thought it a bit peculiar as you're supposed to live alone."

"So you immediately sprang to conclusions. Just like a child."

"I know. I can't be as adult as *you* are about this. Anyway what's it to me if some of your girlfriends sleep over?" She shrugged delicately, amazed she was retaining her poise.

"I can't deny it hasn't happened in the past, Chloe, but it hasn't happened for quite a while. I don't go in for polygamy. It's one woman at a time. The young woman on the phone was my neighbour, Sue Ashton. She and her flatmate, Patrica, had an early morning flight to Sydney. It will connect with a flight to Thailand. They won the trip as a prize but they had to get to Sydney first. I offered to help them carry their luggage down to the car park. I'm always up at that time. Sue and I were coming back up in the lift when you rang. Pat answered the phone, trying to be helpful."

"That's why they've gone to Thailand so they can't confirm it," Chloe said, covering her pain with ice.

"Do you *need* it confirmed? You can't simply believe what I say. You can't trust me?"

"Believing in what men say takes a lot of faith." My God, she thought, on this day of days, I sound awful. Jealousy *was* a sin.

"You mean, believing in *me*, don't you?"

Chloe covered her face with her hands. "I can't think, Gabriel. Too much is happening."

He relented abruptly, putting his own feelings aside. "I can understand that, Chloe. Sit down. The news is wonderful but it must have been quite a shock."

"We did see her smile, Gabriel."

"I think there's some heavenly intervention involved here, Chloe," he said with a gentle wry smile.

She leaned towards him but didn't dare touch him.

"I guess I blundered," she said contritely.

"You did."

"And I apologise." Her breath seemed to be shaking in her throat. She was sure she had lost him. Equally sure she couldn't live with the loss.

"The truth, Chloe, is I have my disappointments, too. I thought our lives had taken a different turn. I thought we were drawing close."

"Of course we were."

"No, not were, *are*. To make a commitment implies trust. You're going to have to decide if you trust me because I desperately want to keep this…friendship, the privilege of knowing you."

In the final analysis, he was the gracious one. "My life is very delicately balanced, Gabriel. It brings its own torments. Hearing a woman's voice at that hour of the morning gave me quite a jolt."

"I expect hearing a man's voice on your phone would do the same for me but I'd have asked to speak to you all the same. Now, let's forget it," he said briskly. Let's ignore the tremendous depth of feeling that has built up between us, he thought. He couldn't deny he was deeply hurt, but he was sorry he had introduced a jarring note. This was Delia's and Chloe's day. A day for joy not for recriminations.

"I'd love to be able to say hello to your mother if I'm able," Gabriel said, his eyes so dark the irises were almost the colour of the pupils.

"I'm sure no one could possibly object." Chloe spoke in a soft, conciliatory tone. "I expect they'll want to run a few tests. Brain scans for sure."

"Your mother is quite coherent?" Gabriel asked. He

realised this was a crucial time; that there might be a relapse.

"She's *herself,* Gabriel. As she used to be, but she is speaking a little strangely."

"How? In what way?" Gabriel said. For the first time he frowned, feeling a lurch of dismay.

"I don't think she wants me to tell another soul."

"I see."

She was acutely conscious she had hurt him.

"No, you *don't* see, Gabriel. I don't want to exclude you. Don't punish me, Gabriel, for a moment's aberration. Total trust doesn't come all that easily. It's just that Mum is talking like she's seen visions."

Gabriel surprised her. "I'm sure she has," he said in a matter-of-fact voice. "Is it a problem, Chloe?"

"Not everyone believes in visions," Chloe said dryly. "Doctors tend to talk more in terms of hallucinatory phenomena. They're a bit negative on things like angels."

"Maybe they haven't got it just right. I know plenty of doctors with strong religious beliefs. Stop worrying now, Chloe. I'm absolutely positive your mother will know how to answer every question that is asked of her."

Which was exactly what happened.

The three of them sat in the summerhouse for an hour after, such a radiance clinging to mother and daughter, Gabriel felt his worldly heart melt. The most beautiful pink rose grew all over the latticed walls of the summerhouse, the essence of its sweet perfume suspended in the golden air. Someone had plucked a single perfect rose and laid it on the table. Delia had gone to it, immediately picked it up, inhaled its scent, as if it had been meant for her, her blue eyes filmed with a quick wash of tears that left them quite brilliant.

She had greeted Gabriel as a welcome stranger, smiling and holding on to his hand. It wasn't until it was time for Chloe and Gabriel to leave that Delia told Gabriel very quietly. "But of course I knew you, Gabriel. You must have been there when my poor old brain let in a chink of light."

It had been decided Delia would be moved to one of the big private hospitals for a few days, taking things quietly, while she underwent a battery of neurological and physical tests, all connected with her total mental, physical and emotional wellbeing.

"I'm going to take you home, Mumma, very soon," Chloe promised. "You'll come through these tests with flying colours."

"I know that, darling," Delia said with sweet composure. "I'll be fine."

When they were in Gabriel's Jaguar about to drive away—Gabriel had decided to have Chloe's car picked up—Delia leaned in the passenger window. "Why don't you say hello to your little brother?"

A *perfect* miracle was too much to hope for. "Because I can't see him, Mumma," Chloe replied, not sure if she was about to sob.

"Turn your head a little to the right, dear. There in the jacaranda. You have to understand Timothy sometimes takes different forms."

"Yes, Mumma." Chloe, seeking to humour her mother, leaned forward and looked out. The jacaranda in full magnificent flower was only a few feet away from the drive. The white gravel was scattered with spent flowers. There was absolutely no one there. No one. Only as Chloe lifted her eyes she saw a pure white dove alight on one of the branches. Its feathers were so *luminous!*

"Look, Gabriel," Chloe said very softly, pointing upwards.

The beautiful dove had disappeared in the twinkling of an eye.

"What's happening?" Chloe asked as they drove away.

"I think we have to accept there's a force at work here, Chloe. A force for the good. It's helping your mother. It's helping you and me. The mother and child we rescued who might have been drowned. I'm not as sceptical as most, I've had my own extreme experience. It changes one's life. I don't reject other people's experiences out of hand. I guess you could say I'm a believer."

"But are the health professionals going to be believers, too?" she asked anxiously. "They might think Mum is still traumatised."

"She's certainly in a state of euphoria," Gabriel had to agree. "She could be hallucinating, Chloe. It could all be an illusion but it's not hurting her or us."

Don't be afraid to trust, Chloe. Don't be afraid to hope.

"Gabriel, did *you* say that?" Chloe asked in a startled voice. Ridiculous question. Gabriel McGuire had long since lost his boy soprano.

"What?" Gabriel shot a glance at Chloe's face. It was full of wonder, but slightly fearful.

"'Don't be afraid to trust, Chloe. Don't be afraid to hope?'" she repeated what she had clearly heard.

"I didn't." He shook his dark head. "But it's very good advice. Take the rest of the day off. It's all been overwhelming. I'll drop you off home, then be on my way."

CHAPTER SEVEN

THE interview with Christopher Freeman was pre-taped on the Tuesday and shown on "Lateline" the following evening. Chloe had declined his dinner invitation as sweetly as she could, but Freeman wasn't about to be put off, claiming it as his due.

"We'll dine at my hotel," he said, naming a very expensive one on the waterfront. The boutique variety. A luxurious home away from home with a very swanky, world-class restaurant.

It shouldn't be any great hardship, Chloe thought.

McGuire thought differently.

"Surely you could have found some excuse to put him off?" His dark, rugged face looked daunting.

Chloe's cheeks tinted slightly. "Look at it this way, Gabriel," Chloe explained patiently. "Something lost, something gained."

"I hope to hell we're not talking about innocence here," he shot back.

"You're being terribly difficult, aren't you?"

"Actually it's like a weight pressing on my heart. I don't like the man, Chloe."

"He came over as absolutely charming on the TV."

"You made him that."

"It's a sort of payback, Gabriel. He did the interview."

"Collected the money."

"He could very well be about to donate it to a shelter for homeless people."

Gabriel shrugged a powerful shoulder. "If he does we'll read about it in the newspapers. No, Chloe,

Freeman, like me, started on the wrong side of the tracks. He knows a great deal more than you and I do about the underbelly of life.''

''You're talking 'underworld'?''

''Not entirely.'' Gabriel looked glum.

''Gabriel, you said it yourself. I'm street smart. We're having dinner in a very posh restaurant in plain public view.''

''The Waverley, where he's staying?'' Gabriel's upward glance was sharp.

''The very same one.''

''What are you wearing?''

Chloe's eyes lit up with amusement, very nearly turquoise like her blouse. ''Gabriel, I wasn't aware you were interested in women's fashions.''

''Not very complimentary,'' he said dryly. ''Of course I'm interested. I always notice what *you* wear.''

''All right, then. I thought black. I have a little short number. Sleeveless, V-neck. A wrap-over dress they call it in the trade. One sensational faux diamond button to fasten it.''

''So you're not going to make it difficult for him?''

''I'll overlook that, McGuire. I'm proud of the way I handle men. At arm's length. He's sending a limo for me. The limo will take me home.''

Gabriel stopped his doodling abruptly. ''Would you like me to ring you? To check you arrive home safely.''

''I don't think that will be necessary. But it's very kind of you,'' she said sweetly.

''Okay, Cavanagh, have your fun. Just don't let that…''

''Steady,'' she warned.

''Get you on a couch.'' His deep vibrant voice had steel in it.

''I think you've forgotten I have a little dynamo packed into this woman's body.''

"I have seen flashes of it." Suddenly he smiled, softening his expression into devastatingly attractive. "Take care, Chloe."

"No *enjoy yourself?*"

"You need *me* with you to do that," he replied provocatively.

Chloe walked to the door, turned back and blew a kiss to him. "I just love you, McGuire."

She looked and sounded radiant as she had done since Delia's miraculous recovery. Gabriel looked after her as she went out of the door and gave a little mocking wave as she passed his windowed wall.

If only it were true.

Chloe looked around the lobby of the Waverley with the greatest of pleasure. The quiet opulence of the decor had enormous appeal for her. Big, beautiful, original oil paintings were placed strategically on the walls. Flower paintings in a marvellous impressionist burst of colour. Chloe had once interviewed the artist in the days when he was up-and-coming. Now he had arrived with an enormous change in his lifestyle. From a flat with no furniture to a lovely old Colonial on the river.

"Miss Cavanagh?" A tall, elegant man came towards her smiling, introducing himself as Dominic Collins, the hotel manager. "Mr. Freeman has asked me to escort you to his suite the moment you arrive."

Suite? Chloe's heart did a back flip. "We're dining in the Victoria Room, is that correct?"

The manager looked surprised. "Mr. Freeman has asked for dinner to be set up in his suite. I've checked everything myself. You won't be disappointed, Miss Cavanagh, I promise you."

There *was* a way out, Chloe knew. Turn around and leave. Only Dominic Collins was gesturing towards the lift that took the most affluent guests to the top floor and one of four luxurious suites.

Christopher Freeman came to the door at the very first tap, his eyes moving over Chloe with extreme admiration.

She was wearing black. He just loved redheads in black. It did marvellous things for her luminous skin. Skin he was dying to stroke. And she looked a little older. More sophisticated than he had yet seen her. He didn't want to be reminded at every turn he was old enough to be her father. Obviously she had worn the little black dress especially to please him.

"Chloe, how perfectly beautiful you look. Do come in. I thought we'd be happier dining in my suite than the main dining room. I like to be out of the public eye at least part of the time. I hope you don't mind." His eyes went momentarily beyond Chloe to the manager. "Many thanks, Collins, for escorting Miss Cavanagh up."

The manager bowed slightly. Not too much. "Everything in order, Mr. Freeman?"

"Everything is splendid!" Freeman enthused. "I'll ring through when we're ready. I think a sip of champagne first."

Chloe had to clear her throat quickly. She moved into the lovely large suite, gazing around with care. The only exit was the balcony and a jolly old drop from there. Gabriel must have made her nervous. Freeman was a man of the world certainly. She didn't suppose he was a rapist.

"Come and sit down, Chloe," he coaxed with his most winning smile. "I want to tell you how pleased I am with our interview. I've had so many phone calls. Everyone seems to think it went over terribly well. I don't always sound so charming, I have to tell you."

"Neither do I." Chloe smiled, as well. She crossed

the large open room, taking her time. The view of the city at night was breathtaking, all the skyscrapers, the tall buildings and towers a dazzle of light. The decor in this particular suite had Art Deco elements, the design of the armchairs and ottomans, the handsome display case filled with pieces of genuine Lalique, the magnificent carpet with its broad bands of cream, deep blue and tan bordered in black. Tiffany lamps stood on the tables and mid-centre of the room a circular dining table had been set up, covered in a white linen-and-lace cloth, and set with the finest crystal, tableware and china. A small arrangement of white orchids was set in the middle, flanked by two silver candlesticks with tall slim tapers. A basket containing a wonderful arrangement of mixed lilies and orchids with tall spiky reeds, dominated a sideboard, in the Art Deco style.

"I expect your friend, McGuire, is worried at your dining alone with me?" Freeman said facetiously.

Chloe smiled. "He can't seem to get through his head you're the perfect gentleman, Christopher."

"Pretty much." He shrugged a dapper shoulder. "Most of the time. I absolutely *love* you in that dress. The hairdo, too. You have a marvellous mane of hair, but the upsweep is very fetching. It shows off your neck and your lovely bone structure." He poured a small amount of champagne into two crystal flutes and offered one to her, taking the other. "Cheers, Chloe. It matters a great deal to me you decided to come. Now what's this about your mother? I want to hear all about it."

At first everything went surprisingly well. Splendid food was wheeled in and out of the suite; food Freeman attacked with gusto and Chloe more sparingly. She was responsible for keeping her petite figure. But what she had was delicious; crab in creamy saffron sauce with a decorative border of golden brown mashed potato, a truly superb honeyed-ginger duck and a fruit mould served with brandied cream. Just a taste.

"Let's have coffee out on the balcony," Christopher suggested. "It's a beautiful night." Indeed it was. The city spread out in a glitter of light. Above them, the velvet black sky shimmered with a trillion stars. Chloe wondered what Gabriel was doing. Night-time was always so romantic. She would never cease to be amazed at how rapidly their relationship had changed. He had only to kiss her to strip away her defences. Only to kiss her for her to open her eyes and her heart.

"Chloe?" Freeman came up behind her as she leaned against the railing. "What are you thinking about?" he asked seductively, pretty well used to instant success.

How could she say, "Gabriel"? Only Gabriel had ever sent that all-powerful surge of longing through her veins. "Just admiring the view, Christopher," she said lightly. "The city skyline has changed so much of recent years."

"It has indeed," he responded kindly, when his New York penthouse overlooked the incredible drama of Manhattan. "I don't think you realise, Chloe…" He paused to slip his arm around her tiny waist. He wasn't a big man so he preferred his women small and light-limbed. "But I'm falling a little in love with you."

How ghastly. And I did this to myself, Chloe thought.

"I suppose you say that to all the girls, Christopher?" She confronted him with a gentle ironic smile.

Keep cool now. Keep your head. It's important at this point.

Was that the voice again or just her head buzzing?

"Sure I do." He laughed. "Only this time I mean it."

It won't help. "I was hoping you'd tell me about how you brought off the Avalon/Mercer merger," she said in a bright, intensely interested tone.

"You want to talk business on a night like this?" he scoffed.

"Christopher, I wouldn't hurt you for the world. I very much appreciate your giving me an exclusive interview. It was a considerable coup but I'm not into...dalliance, if that's what this is."

For the first time he looked taken aback, staring at her in unfeigned surprise.

"Chloe, you little devil, are you talking marriage?" As a suggestion, it wasn't half bad. She was young. She was beautiful. Highly intelligent, but not the genius he was. She was, in short, a little sweetheart.

Now it was Chloe's turn to be surprised. "The thought never entered my mind."

Christopher smiled at her, taking pleasure in their little game. "Confess you've considered it. I'm what's known as a marvellous catch."

"I'm sure of it, Christopher. *Every time.*"

"You don't like the idea I've been married before?" he asked anxiously.

"I know a lot of people do it. All the time."

Freeman grinned. "Like Liz and me. We're always looking for that perfect partner."

Keep looking, Chloe thought, but spoke sweetly. "I don't want to risk damaging our pleasant acquaintance, Christopher. I've so enjoyed meeting you but I'm not thinking of marriage for a very long time."

She went to turn away, but he reacted quickly, pulling her into his arms. "Maybe you need a little something to convince you," he said, and then laughed impishly.

Chloe fought an irresistible urge to hit him. Wipe the silly smile off his face. Did he *really* think she was playing games?

"Everything will be fine if you'd only relax," he said in a cajoling voice.

"Christopher, please stop." Chloe could feel the heat

of anger in her face but he laughed again, his early warning system hopelessly awry.

Freeman genuinely thought Chloe was teasing him. It had been a very long time, perhaps twenty years since a woman had rejected him. Why, he had read in countless women's magazines he was terribly attractive. His mirror told him the same.

"Well, I don't mind a little tussle if you don't." He smiled.

"I think not!" Chloe felt like a total idiot. "I really should be going." Just to prove the point she wrenched herself out his arms, preparing herself for a very quick getaway. She knew exactly where she had left her evening purse.

Something wasn't right, Freeman thought. He made a grab for her, intending to start all over again, more slowly this time, only he heard the sudden pop of a button, saw its sparkle against the black border of the carpet. It couldn't have been him. He couldn't have torn her dress. Why, that button was barely sewn on.

Three things happened at once.

Freeman, as near to shocked as he could be, endeavoured to pull Chloe back into his arms, anxious to placate her, perhaps scoop her up. She was a featherweight. He should be able to do it, besides he had a little present for her, a diamond tennis bracelet. Chloe, however, turned on him like a tiny fury, pushing him back, and then there was a very loud rap on the door.

"Who the devil is that?" Freeman cursed savagely, hopping about nursing the knee he had struck against the timber frame of the Art Deco armchair. He thought he was fresh out of surprises, but that little girl could very likely beat him, if it ever came to a fight.

"It shouldn't have been like this," Chloe was saying, trying to gather her open wrap dress together while she dashed to the door at high speed.

She threw it open, just knowing it had to be Gabriel.

"I *knew* it was you!" she cried, staring up at his tall, powerful figure. His eyes were glittering like jet, his cleft chin very pronounced.

"How very touching!" He took in her disarray with one furious glance. The milky slope of her small breasts, the low cut of a black lace bra, the bare midriff and glimpses of very small black lacy briefs and the sheerest stockings. He couldn't look any more. Enough that he was here. He'd been almost asleep watching an old Humphrey Bogart movie when a voice had jerked him back to wakefulness.

Chloe needs you.

A great anger overtook him, now flooding him with rage. Just this once Freeman was going to get what he deserved.

He put Chloe aside like a rag doll and started towards Freeman.

With the swiftness of sheer desperation, Christopher got behind the dining table ready to overturn it if he had to. He knew if McGuire landed just one punch on him he would surely lay him out, McGuire looked that bad. Like an avenging angel, eyes blazing, power radiating from his imposing body.

"Gabriel, Gabriel, he didn't do anything," Chloe blurted out, switching from high relief to panic.

"Did he not?" Gabriel slowed for an instant to allow his eyes to whip over her again. She looked so incredibly desirable it was like a blade to his heart.

"Wake up, McGuire." The plea was thick in Freeman's voice. "Let her speak."

Not for the first time Chloe blessed her miraculous turn of speed. She was somehow between them, half pummelling, half pushing Gabriel back. Her beautiful red-gold hair had escaped its roll, flying freely around her white face. "I lost the button on my dress, Gabriel.

That's all. Embarrassing, I know. It couldn't have been sewn on properly.''

"Do you think I'm stupid?'' Gabriel frowned ferociously on her.

"Well, I can tell you it would be pretty stupid to assault me,'' Freeman croaked.

McGuire laughed scornfully. "Maybe you wouldn't like the story to get out, either.'' He endeavoured to get past Chloe but Chloe checked him with a single hand.

"Stop that, Chloe,'' Gabriel snapped, resigned to her miraculous feats of strength.

"We should talk. Just let me sew the button on.''

"I'm absolutely certain I saw a little sewing kit in a drawer,'' Freeman piped up helpfully. "I can understand your jumping to the wrong conclusion, McGuire. What I can't understand is why you're here.''

"I had a call,'' Gabriel stated bluntly.

"Oh, really?'' Freeman's voice was flat with disbelief. He pressed his hands down on the white tablecloth, tremendously grateful the table was there between them. "Why so emotional anyway? Why this excess of aggression? You're not married to Chloe, are you? Not engaged?''

"Looking after her is getting to be a big part of my job,'' Gabriel said, quite literally stuck to the spot.

"It's all a mistake, Gabriel.'' Chloe gave him a sweet little kitten's smile. She pushed needle and cotton through the button and finished off beautifully.

"I'm shocked that you'd think otherwise,'' Freeman added virtuously. "I have the greatest regard for Chloe.'' He took a deep breath. "Why I even asked her to become my wife,'' he lied.

A mad, ironic laugh burbled out of McGuire. "Is this true, Chloe?''

"I think I could have managed it had I pushed.'' Chloe was fixing her hair as fast as she could.

"Christopher, thank you for dinner, but I think we should be on our way."

"If you must," Christopher all but whimpered with relief. Back in New York he had minders but no one seemed to think much of them here.

Only then did Gabriel seem able to move. "I don't think you've got anything left to say to Chloe?" He flashed Freeman a black challenge.

"Only that it's been a great pleasure meeting her. I don't think I can say the same for you, McGuire. As it happens I have to be back in New York by the end of the week."

"Well, bon voyage," Gabriel said.

Outside in the corridor, McGuire got back his strength. He put a hand beneath Chloe's elbow and all but lifted her to the elevator. On the ground floor he trotted her to his car, parked where it shouldn't have been in the circular drive, but no one appeared to have noticed or had any objection. He opened the passenger door, tucked her in, all the while burning with frustration.

Inside the comforting cocoon of the Jaguar, Chloe shook her head from side to side trying to absorb it all. Apparently she had flashes of superhuman strength. It could make a great story, only she didn't want the publicity. Even allowing for this strength, how come she had held Gabriel off so easily? It was odd. Very odd.

Gabriel slid behind the wheel, the expression on his rugged face as puzzled as hers. "Do you want to tell me the *real* story?"

"I thought I did."

"Oh, come off it, Chloe. I don't think I'll ever get over the fact you're so strong."

"For very short bursts of time," she pointed out fairly hastily.

"I don't know." Gabriel shook his head. "Maybe it's

a spell." He laughed at himself. "Maybe it's a kind of hypnosis. What the hell's your secret?"

"I don't know," Chloe answered in a quiet, worried voice. "I'm not on medication. I'm not even convinced it's *me*."

Gabriel laughed again. "You're getting a little help on the side."

"It's the only explanation I can come up with. Anyway you're not telling why *you* drove out into the night. And what was that about a call? I didn't call."

"What difference does it make?" He shrugged. "I arrived. You looked pretty damned upset when I did. I should have flattened that creep."

"Then we could all get our pictures in the papers. No, Gabriel. I *had* to stop you."

"God, I must be the biggest chump that ever lived," he groaned. "Stopped by a redhead who doesn't come up to my shoulder. It wasn't very smart of you, either, wearing that dress."

"I wanted to look a bit more sophisticated."

"I mean, under the dress you couldn't have worn *less*," he said in a shocked tone.

"Oh, go to hell, McGuire." Chloe's voice rose a little. "Why were you *looking* anyway?"

"Chloe, Chloe, the temptation was too great. You looked straight out of a male fantasy. Black lace bra, tiny little briefs, sheer black stockings. I thought nice girls wore petticoats?"

"Well, you're mistaken," she said tartly. "As if it's any of your business. This dress is fully lined. It makes the wearing of a slip unnecessary. Besides, a slip would show when I sat down."

"But why stir Freeman up?" Gabriel persisted. "Wasn't he already stirred up enough?"

"Sure, and *you* aren't?"

"That's because you know all the buttons to push," he said with a remote kind of mocking.

"Don't let's talk any more." Chloe looked out the window. "I don't remember asking you to come rescue me but thanks for the lift home."

Neither said a word from there on in. McGuire insisted on seeing her into the house, circling around, lifting the curtains.

"I don't know what I'd do without you," Chloe taunted. "What would you actually do if someone fell out of the drapes?"

"Me?" His handsome face twisted. "I'd do nothing. I'd leave it all up to you."

"So would you like a cup of coffee?" she relented.

"If you can't think of anything else?"

"What is that supposed to mean?" She swung back, her heart giving a hot little leap. He was wearing a black T-shirt with beige trousers. The tightness of the T-shirt showed off his splendid torso and the strength of his arms. He was wearing his hair longer, too. She supposed she had started it by saying what great hair he had so why did he get it cut so short? The result was a magnificent head of crisp jet-black waves. Mediterranean hair. Mediterranean appearance. Except he was very much taller than the norm. There had to be Greek or Italian in his background.

"So why are you staring at me?" he asked in a defensive voice.

"Well, why not?" she retorted. "You're a very handsome man."

"You mean it's taken you all this time to find out." His black gaze was ironic.

"No, but I used to think very dark powerful-looking men weren't to my taste."

"Tell me something I don't know," he softly jeered. "May I ask the type you *do* admire?"

"You're looking at him," Chloe said simply.

That stopped McGuire.

"That photograph of my father on the piano," she indicated. There were in fact a dozen photographs in silver frames on the closed lid of an ebony grand. Gabriel moved towards the piano and picked up a photograph of a handsome man in his early forties. Fine distinguished features. Ash-blond hair, grey eyes, a very attractive mouth of generous proportions. Chloe's mouth. Otherwise she closely resembled her mother.

"Your father was a patrician," Gabriel said with genuine feeling.

Chloe went to him and stood by his shoulder. "His name was Peter. A better man would be hard to find. I loved him with all my heart. Loved and admired him. He was so clever. Destined for great things. Then he was killed."

"That's the way the cards are dealt, Chloe," Gabriel sighed. As he went to put the photograph down, a standard 8x10, Gabriel fancied he saw another face superimposed on Peter Cavanagh's. His whole body went still as he stared. Red-gold hair, big blue eyes, a sprinkling of freckles across a cute nose. A boy of around eight. A boy who looked very much like Chloe. A second passed and the illusion, more like a trick of the light, disappeared.

"So when are they going to allow your mother to come home?" Gabriel asked as he followed Chloe into the kitchen.

"We're looking at the weekend. Even the doctors are talking a miracle."

"I must think of seeing my mother," Gabriel said. "Life is so short."

"Can't you treat her to a holiday? Her and your aunt?" Chloe asked.

"Of course I can," he said in frustration. "I *want* to.

The difficulty is getting my mum to agree. Don't let's say any more about it, Chloe. It hurts me.''

''I'm so sorry, Gabriel. I just want you to know I understand how you feel.''

''Do you?'' He looked at her with a kind of fierce tenderness.

''I know the pain in you.'' She reached out without thought, tracing the outline of his disturbing mouth. Such a yearning was in her, a yearning that had been smouldering since the first time he had kissed her. All she had to do was touch him for excitement to flare like a spark in dry grass.

''Chloe?'' he said.

''Gabriel,'' she answered him, watching hypnotically while he put his arm around her waist, drew her to him. ''If I don't go home now,'' he said very tightly, ''I'm taking you to bed.''

Chloe stared into the taut dark face looming over her, the features not sculpted but hewn. She could sense the frustrated passion in him, the protectiveness that plagued him. In a moment she was certain he could put her violently away from him. It couldn't happen. Not when she wanted him so desperately. She had lived with loneliness too long. Now she wanted the shelter of this man's arms around her. His passionate love. Obeying her instincts, Chloe allowed her body to settle into his. It was a rapturous feeling, enormously soothing yet blissfully sensual. Her eyelids closed even as her mouth opened to his wild, heart-shaking kiss.

Could she live up to such passion? This magnificent tide of desire that left her enmeshed in a pleasure beyond all imagining.

''Chloe, I want you so badly.'' His hard-muscled body was shaking with the force of it. Was she simply falling in love with love? Wanting love so desperately to make up for the years of deprivation. He felt like pouring out his soul to her but if he didn't keep something back he knew he could be very badly hurt.

She was so light. Like a drift of apple blossom. The radiance that was in her streamed from her mouth. She was *Woman*. He lifted her, not sure what he was doing, not wanting to shock her. Maybe they were hopelessly unsuited? Mismatched? Beauty and the Beast, he thought wryly even as a kind of anger prowled in him. He knew under his granite exterior he was an emotional being. Why didn't he stick to his usual women, women who knew their way around the world? Gabriel didn't realise he was rocking her, standing in the kitchen rocking her like a baby, her curly head burrowed against his chest.

Any minute now that mystery wind would blow up, blustering headlong through the house, sending curtains flying and ornaments toppling over.

After a few minutes of waiting, Gabriel realised it wasn't going to be one of those nights. There was no one and nothing to break the spell.

"Chloe?" He looked down at her snuggled in his arms.

"Don't go away. Don't leave me," she said in a trembly voice.

"I don't think I can." His tone was half tender, half despairing.

"Do I have to lead you to my bedroom?" She reached up and clasped her arms tightly behind his neck.

He cut her short. "Chloe, this is for *real*. You *do* see that? I want you more than I've ever wanted anything in this world. If I start to make love to you there's no *going back*."

She got a good firm hold on him. "You don't have to treat me as though I'm crushable, Gabriel. I want you, too. I want to identify with you, body and soul. You're not luring me. I'm luring you." She had to make an effort to overcome his scruples. He had to be among the last men in the world to have them.

"So be it!" Gabriel said while the front door quietly opened and shut as if someone had gone out.

In the quiet of her lovely bedroom, Gabriel undressed her with exquisite delicacy. She was so absolutely the opposite of him, so small, so soft, so full of grace with her fragile bones and the incredibly silky quality of her skin; skin that had the freshness of spring flowers. He had expected to find a certain tenseness, perhaps apprehension, from her altered breathing, but she was responding with a glorious eagerness and ardency, a trust in him as her lover. Her *first* lover. Nothing could change that. He wanted it to be a beautiful, unforgettable experience, one that she would remember every time she closed her eyes.

A late moon had risen, riding high in the sky, flooding the bedroom with a silvery light.

If I live to be a hundred, these moments would always remain with me, Chloe thought. She was totally disarmed by the tenderness of Gabriel's lovemaking. It had such *meaning* to it, yet she felt the force of his sexuality right down to her marrow. His marvellous hands shaped her body, keenly exploring its delicate construction, so different yet so complementary to his own. She had to arch her back in ecstasy. Her bedroom was a temple. The moon was at the window transmitting its luminous beams. Such rapture was pouring into her like a torrent and all from Gabriel's worshipful mouth and hands.

Once he bent his head to question her and she answered shyly, giving him the liberty to bring her tremulous yearning body to full readiness. Every nerve in her body was a string of some wondrous instrument played with harmony and power by a master hand. Innocent that she was, Chloe didn't know she was giving the depth of her own feelings their fullest expression.

At a certain moment she cried out, disturbed by a sudden spear of pain, then the wonderful ripples began, the scarcely-to-be-borne glorious stream of excitement that rolled in, in fuller and fuller waves, gathering her up in its mighty motion until it left her on the sublime shore of Heaven, locked in Gabriel's embrace.

CHAPTER EIGHT

IT WAS a wonderful day when Chloe brought her mother home. Gabriel was going to visit later but he hadn't wanted to intrude on this very special time when Delia returned to the peace and the privacy of her own house.

Surprisingly, though it was very emotional, there was no sense of grief, just the silent acknowledgment that Delia's husband and Chloe's father had gone, never to live with them again. Both women felt very much as though Peter accompanied them in spirit. They stood in the brilliant sunlight admiring the garden which somehow had sprung overnight into full glorious bloom. Great masses of white and blue agapanthus tightly furled the day before, showed magnificent full heads. The white Iceberg rose was flowering more profusely than ever, but what was most extraordinary, the garden beds that flanked the front step and ran the full length of the house to either side, were thick with tall, gleaming white lilies; the lilies her mother loved and Chloe had never seen flower all the time her mother had been in the nursing home.

"Oh, darling, I've missed it all so!" Delia exclaimed, her arm wrapped around her daughter's waist. "You've kept everything so beautifully. How did you do it when you've had to work so hard?"

Chloe was very much at a loss to say how. Although she had kept everything as neat as she possibly could, turning the garden to native low maintenance, here it was looking absolutely spectacular with a massed display of perennials. That at least was explainable, but she was certain she had pulled out all the annuals because she simply didn't have the time to replace them. Yet there they were in wonderful combinations of colour.

"Shall we go into the house, darling." Delia drew a deep breath of satisfaction. "I'd love a cup of tea."

Over the next few days, Chloe was immensely grateful her mother had settled in so well. Delia had several devoted friends who had kept up with her progress through thick and thin, visiting her in the nursing home, bringing little gifts and flowers, no matter their old Delia didn't know them, now their telephone calls came through to Delia herself. They were overjoyed for her, told her repeatedly what a wonderful daughter she had and begged to visit when Delia was properly settled in.

In the old days Delia with her distinguished physician husband had been invited everywhere. They had very many friends. Now Delia knew who were the true friends.

For Chloe it was a hectic time getting her outfit together for the Turf Racing Carnival on the following Saturday. As a judge and TV presenter she had to look good. Money was no option. The channel was paying for her to be outfitted from head to toe. Gabriel had given her carte blanche.

In the end it came down to two designer suits. One, white in a summer-weight wool and silk mix, the jacket, the hem of the short skirt and the collar of the button-fronted little vest piped in black. Her shoes were white with a black trim; a wonderful wide-brimmed black hat that really made a statement. Or, a bright pink suit with a longer split at the front skirt, a beautifully fitting collarless jacket with gold buttons over a rose-printed pink silk camisole and again a lovely big hat adorned with a crush of roses, very chic pink sandals colour-matched to her suit. Both of the outfits looked so good, everyone including the young designer had difficulty making a final choice.

"I'll bring my boss in," Chloe offered, holding out the pink jacket to an assistant. "He has excellent taste and the station *is* paying for it."

But Chloe couldn't get Gabriel that day. He was closeted with two "Big Shot Americans" definitely in the industry, who appeared to have known Gabriel when he was stationed in Washington.

"He was a star in the making," Jennifer, standing by Chloe's desk, told her. "Gabe told me he loved his time in the United States. He claimed he learned everything he knows there."

"He still wanted to come home," Chloe said, knowing a moment of sheer fright.

"You know perfectly well Gabe's on a different level from the rest of us," Jennifer answered scornfully. "He's not running to his full potential."

"I agree." Chloe spoke in a subdued voice that wasn't lost on Jennifer. "I think his stint here is only a stepping stone. A kind of springboard to higher things."

"Personally," said Jennifer with some relish. "I believe he could be off to greener pastures. He's not the boardroom type, is he? He's an out there and at 'em kind of guy. A dynamo. I shouldn't be surprised if we get a shock announcement. He's going back to the States. He even managed to get a bit of an accent when he was there."

"It's a cosmopolitan voice," Chloe said.

"True. He's a big man with a big role to fill, so don't get too fond of him, Cavanagh." Jennifer gave Chloe a taut smile. "I'm really pleased to hear about your mother. You wouldn't want to leave her."

Impossible to leave her, Chloe thought, as Jennifer moved off. Delia was gaining strength and balance every day but Chloe couldn't deny her mother's trauma hadn't changed her. Not a lot of people carried on conversations with the little son they had lost. Now that she thought about it, Chloe realised she wasn't all that "normal" herself, hearing voices as she did from time to time.

Quite a few of her colleagues took time out to enquire about her mother and pass a remark about McGuire's visitors.

"I hope they're not trying to talk him into going back to the States," Bob said, looking quite downcast. "He's the best boss we've ever had. We need a strong guy running things. We might have been a bit anxious when he arrived. It took a while to get used to his style after poor old Clive, now we're all so supportive. Even *you*, Chloe."

Chloe nodded emphatically. She couldn't speak for the lump in her throat.

"I guess he's too damned young, too great-looking, to stay *behind* the camera," Bob mused. "There must have been a lot of excitement in his life working over there. I mean, we're talking about the most dynamic, the most powerful country in the world. Gabe's such a force himself."

"We'll know soon enough, Bob," Chloe cast a glance in the direction of Gabriel's office. "By the way, I've got a couple of outfits picked out for Saturday. You're still going to photograph the whole thing?"

"Chloe, love, could you get anyone better?" Bob asked. "So what *is* the look?"

"Smart, exclusive, definitely the outfit to wear to a big race meeting. One's pink, the other's white."

"You'll look great in both." Bob turned to walk away, then paused. "Poor old Jen has her nose out of joint. She used to do these Fashion on the Field events."

"I know." Chloe gave a heartfelt sigh. "I know she's

hurt but I didn't have anything to do with being asked, Bobby.''

"Well, love, you've got it all over Jen, haven't you? She's a good dresser and she *is* attractive, but not a patch on you. Sponsors want the best every time. I'm just sorry Jen's got so sharp-tongued. She shouldn't call attention to the fact she's so jealous.''

"It can't be easy being passed over." Chloe realised in time it would happen to her. "All I can say is, I don't deliberately stand on other people's toes.''

"Course you don't, love. You're as sweet as you're beautiful. There's Gabe now." Bob looked down the corridor. "He's showing his pals out. Or he could be going out to lunch with them. He's putting his jacket on.''

Lunch it was. Gabriel left the message with Amanda at reception.

It wasn't until late afternoon that Chloe got a call to see Gabriel in his office. She sat down in the chair opposite him waiting for him to speak. Gabriel on the job wasn't the same person who had made love to her, turning her whole life inside out. At the station, Gabriel was *McGuire,* very much her boss, the man who had single-handedly brought BTQ8 to the top of the ratings, a man much admired in the field of television news.

His dark head was downbent as he studied some printed page in front of him, something he found very interesting because his concentration was genuine and intense. He was wearing a blue-striped Oxford shirt with a red silk tie with a small pattern in white and navy, the colours accentuating his dark golden skin and, as he looked up, his very white attractive smile.

"So how's it going, Cavanagh?"

She decided to respond blithely, hiding her concerns. "I managed to get a few moments with Elle Macpherson before she attended the sneak preview of her new movie, plus a quote from George Clooney. There had to be at least a hundred international television, radio and print journalists all fighting me to get to them. George is gorgeous and the fans were going wild. Everyone loves Elle, but I have to tell you pandemonium broke loose when Clooney arrived. Women were weeping and fainting.''

"You're kidding!"

"No way. You had to see it to believe it. Anyway our shoot will be on the news tonight. Elle was wearing a sensational pink Valentino. No wonder they call her The Body. Which reminds me. We're having difficulty picking which outfit I'll wear on Saturday. Both of them look good. I thought if you had a minute you could make the final choice.''

"Sure." He didn't even hesitate. "I'd be delighted to. Brad Devine has pulled out of the judging at almost the last minute. Some gig he can't get out of so the organisers have asked me to take his place.''

Chloe felt an upthrust of pleasure. "That's great. You can keep me company.''

"That's the intention." He smiled. "How's Delia?"

"She's settling in better than I ever thought possible. Her old friends are ringing her, wanting to visit. For the moment though she's content to enjoy being home and wandering around the garden.''

"So?" Gabriel studied her, seeing the wry light in her eyes.

"She's still talking to Tim," Chloe confided quietly.

Gabriel's shapely mouth curved. "These days I'd have to say he's probably around. Don't worry about it, Chloe. If it helps your mother it's doing no harm.''

"No." She sounded unconvinced. "I hope you don't mind if I ask this?''

"Ask away. I don't have to answer," Gabriel mocked.

"How did lunch go with your American friends?''

Gabriel speared a hand through his thick jet-black hair, so a crisp wave fell onto his broad forehead. It gave him a very attractive, rakish look. "One of them is the president of a top TV station," he explained. "The other is the New York reporter, Joe Costello. Joe's won all the big awards in his time, made the covers of all the magazines."

"So what did they want with you?" Chloe asked, aware it had come out much too abruptly.

He shrugged. "Believe it or not, Chloe, they want me for their news team. Joe in particular remembers me from my years in Washington."

"When were you going to tell me?" Chloe cursed herself as soon as she said it. Who did she think she was, his wife?

"Chloe, we've been both tied up all afternoon until now," he answered mildly.

"I'm sorry." Chloe was beginning to feel very unsure of herself, close to abandonment.

"There's no need to be sorry, Chloe. I'm telling as few people as possible. Of course that doesn't include you. What I want to know is how do *you* feel?"

"About the possibility of your going back to the States?"

"That, too."

Her lashes veiled her eyes. "I would never deny you your big chance, Gabriel. You deserve every success. A bigger career than you've got now."

He was silent for a moment. "Chloe, this is only the beginning. I always intended to put BTQ8 back on the map before I moved on. I love challenges. I thrive on them."

"You're really a reporter at heart, aren't you? An investigative reporter. Clever and dedicated enough to get to the bottom of the toughest story."

"I enjoyed that part of my life, Chloe," he replied.

"And it's not over." Chloe was feeling more and more alone.

"I need a chance to think. I can see from your expression you might miss me?" Gabriel asked.

"Maybe I would." Chloe sat perfectly straight.

"You couldn't think of coming with me?"

Chloe could feel her heart give a painful lurch. "No, Gabriel. I can't leave my mother. She's been given a second chance at life but I don't think she's truly over all the things that have happened to her. Probably never will be."

"You mean, because she says all these strange things?"

Chloe nodded, lowering her blue eyes. "It's beautiful but it's terrifying, too. I have to be on hand, Gabriel. You can understand that?"

"Of course I can," he answered a little harshly. "I know you'd deny your own chance at happiness to be there for your mother."

"My mother is part of my happiness," she insisted.

"Chloe, I understand perfectly." He never moved his dark eyes from her face. "We've come a long way, haven't we?"

It was impossible to deny. "I'm not sure that I haven't fallen a little in love with you," Chloe said. She had to turn her head away to say it. *A little?* When he'd taken her over in every way. Central to everything was her deep-seated fear of loss. Maybe she would *never* feel safe and secure. She had always known, too, her relationship with Gabriel McGuire carried an element of danger.

"But you still find it impossible to trust me?"

"Explain. In what way?"

"You've been too vulnerable for too long, Chloe," he said. "Falling in love can be shattering. It *is*. Do you really think I haven't formed a considerable emotional attachment to you?''

Chloe felt a surge of anger. ''I know you could break it, Gabriel, if you had to. On your own admission you're highly ambitious.''

''I've already suggested we needn't be parted.''

''Join you? On what basis, live-in lovers? Pay attention. I can't leave Mum on her own. For all the miracle of her recovery, I still wake up every morning wondering how long it's going to last.''

''You have to have *faith*, Chloe,'' he told her, his expression intense.

''I don't have *that* kind of faith, Gabriel. I know all the terrible things that can happen. Anyway, we haven't got to the point of making any deep commitment to one another.''

His own temper flashed. ''*Haven't* we?''

''Well, *I* haven't.'' Chloe lifted her chin, her eyes huge and vividly blue.

''I'm sorry, Chloe.'' He shook his head. ''I know you too well. You let me love you and it *was* love. Not sex.''

''It was fantastic.'' Even that was an inadequate word.

''And totally meaningful. I haven't made any decision, Chloe. I'm not threatening our relationship. I'm only letting you know what's happening in my life. I know you'll keep it private.''

Chloe, the redhead, shot up out of her chair. ''That was completely unnecessary, McGuire,'' she flared.

His look was wry. ''Well, I know it was. Actually I was just...''

''Filling in time?''

''Calm yourself, Chloe,'' he said acidly. ''You're going to have to do some mellowing before you get yourself a husband.''

''Well, one thing's certain, I couldn't stay married long to *you*.''

"I haven't asked you, for a start.   There was an answering glint in his coal black eyes.

"What would be the point if you're heading straight for the States?" She spoke quite loudly, causing him to wince.

"Keep your voice down, Cavanagh. Is that all right with you?"

"I'm sorry." She apologised immediately.

"Why don't we have something to eat later?" he suggested in a more amiable tone. "Or we could take it home to be with Delia."

"Thanks for the kind offer but I've got all kinds of things to do," she snapped.

"Like what?"

Chloe flushed. "I'm going to make a great big casserole. A hearty Italian stew, Hunter's style. Something that will keep us going for a week."

He laughed. "I could help you slice the onions."

"I'm afraid, no. I'm someone who believes in only one cook to a kitchen. Is there anything else or may I go?"

Gabriel placed his hands in a steeple beneath his cleft chin, studying her. "Cavanagh, you're taking me right back to the early days when you were such an uppity little thing."

She raised her delicate winged brows. "Maybe we'll start to feel bad about one another again."

"Not *me,* Cavanagh," he confirmed bluntly. "You, I like. Now—" Gabriel consulted his desk calendar "—I can fit you in tomorrow about ten-twenty, ten-thirty."

"Fit me in for what?" she asked in haughty puzzlement.

"Let's start all over again. Aren't *you* the one who asked *me* to help you with your outfit?"

"Oh!" Chloe stood there looking angry and injured

and quite, quite beautiful. "You don't really have to bother."

"Do you mind?" he said with a laconic inflection. "The station is paying for this. I do have to bother. Ten-twenty in this office, and can you take this pile of blurb down to Ray Hope and tell him to put it through the shredder and start again."

"You don't have to be nasty," Chloe said, taking charge of Ray's news story.

"I can't see being kind is going to do it. I'm the boss, Cavanagh. It might pay you to remember it."

Gabriel took less than a minute the next day to make the final decision on her outfit. "The white and black," he said confidently. "I'm just crazy about that hat."

"So what's wrong with the pink?" Chloe asked.

"It's lovely but it's more like a garden party. The other is pure race glamour. Trust me on this one, Cavanagh."

When they arrived at the course the following Saturday, Chloe was delighted she had.

"You look perfect. Absolutely perfect," the Chairman of the Turf Club told her enthusiastically, a connoisseur of thoroughbreds. "You're going to have the devil of a day trying to pick winners, dear. I haven't seen so many good-looking, well-dressed contestants in a long while. Best of luck."

Chloe had already caught a glimpse of Tara Williams, resplendent in a fire-engine-red suit, the skirt of which was only one step away from a micromini, with a huge red-banded black hat adorned with a big red-and-black ribbon-bow centre front. Chloe as yet didn't know if Tara was going to be one of the contestants. Anything to get herself on TV, Chloe thought. There were plenty of white outfits, more of pink. Pink in all shades seemed to be the in-colour. A stunning lime green number with a lovely white hat bordered in the same green. A truly terrible polka dot outfit that seemed to faze the eye, and a very chic orange ensemble spoiled by the fact the white and orange hat was worn too far back on the head.

Gabriel was the big surprise, resplendent in tails and a pearl grey topper, with a beautiful blue-and-silver tie and a white carnation in his buttonhole.

"You're continually surprising me, Gabriel," Chloe said, staring up at him in open-mouthed admiration. He looked wonderful, the most dashing man there.

"You little snob." His brilliant black eyes gleamed.

"I don't mean to be, truly. That's awful to say that."

"You're exceptionally snobbish," he said, determined to take a rise out of her. "But you look just beautiful. I really know how to pick an outfit."

"At least let me share in it. Where's Bob?"

"He's circulating. That's his job. You can float around looking exquisite while you're waiting to chat up all the socialities pretending not to notice the camera." Gabriel, from his vantage point of six-three looked over the head of the large crowd. "Was that Tara I saw minus her skirt?"

Chloe laughed then. "It's terribly short, isn't it? Too short isn't elegant."

"It's not bad when you've got racehorse legs."

"Are you saying my legs are too short?" Chloe clutched at her large hat as the breeze threatened to get under it.

"Let's put it this way. They're not too short for your body."

"I get the feeling you're teasing."

"How well you know me."

In the end it was a lot of fun, the large crowd cheering and clapping when the winner was announced, Miss Katy Nugent, in the lime green outfit. Tara, who had been a contestant, stalked up to Chloe, her lips tightly pursed. How she had missed out on first prize when her outfit was far and away the most stunning and her father owned the station, was beyond her. Her whole attitude let everyone in the vicinity know she'd been wronged.

"I might have known, seeing you're involved," she hissed at Chloe.

"All fair and square, Tara?" Chloe shook her head. "You look striking, but Katy's outfit was the big crowd pleaser. Three out of the four judges picked it."

"I bet Gabe didn't." Tara tossed her head.

"I'd rather not say. That would spoil things. I'm sorry you're disappointed."

"I am pretty angry," Tara agreed grumpily. "Personally I thought the green outfit looked like she made it herself."

Chloe just smiled back, further enraging Tara. "Of course you must be feeling pretty damned disappointed yourself," she said, pulling a face.

"Actually, I feel on top of the world," Chloe countered, knowing something distasteful was coming.

"Well, yes, about your mother. That's great news," Tara had the grace to say, "but you must have heard Gabe looks like leaving us. Ah, that wiped the smile off your face."

Chloe's small frame stiffened. "How did you know?"

Tara didn't know. She had overheard her father speculating with someone on the phone. It was no secret Gabe had been visited by American media people. "Gabe told me, of course," Tara lied. "I guess he owed me that. After all, we were lovers at one time." She stared at Chloe through narrowed lids.

"That's news to me, Tara." She had to learn to *trust* some time.

"There are lots of things about Gabe you don't know." Tara's gaze slid across Chloe's face with a mixture of pity and triumph. "Bye, bye, now don't let me spoil your day."

Well she did try.

Chloe didn't confront Gabriel when he returned to her side. He was in excellent spirits, handing her a list he'd jotted down.

"What's this?" she asked as they walked up the steps to the stand.

"I'm no punter, but today I'm backing any horse whose name has even a remote connection with *Angel*. I've just won a thousand dollars on a rank outsider, Mysterious." He laughed.

"That's wonderful!" Chloe exclaimed, sitting down and beginning to read. "Hail to All, Little Angel, Proud Guardian and Heavenly Prince." She turned to him, trying hard to thrust every doubt from her mind. "We have to bet on something, I suppose. The only race I follow is the Melbourne Cup."

"Along with everyone else in the country. So what's it to be? I've got five minutes to put our money on Hail to All."

Every last horse on Gabriel's list ran a place.

Chloe was in the paddock watching the runners for the last race parading, when the beautiful bright chestnut gelding, Solar Gold, race ready and in peak condition, was suddenly spooked by a flying object. It turned out to be a woman's hat. The breeze was coming in stiff gusts now, dislodging the offending hat that all but landed at the gelding's feet. All might have been well, the young woman strapper who had been leading the horse was well experienced, but she just as suddenly sneezed violently from the flying dust, lost control of the reins and fell backwards. The magnificent animal, turned out to perfection and hyped up to race, reared. Power ripped through its muscles from shoulder to haunch. The strapper managed to roll away but before anyone could sort themselves out, Chloe who had belonged to a pony club for most of her childhood, was propelled into action. Instead of standing well back as everyone else around the ring was doing, she slipped through the opening, holding up her arms grasping for the reins, all the while talking to Solar Gold in a soothing secret language made up of little bitty clicks, a snatch of song, and some very odd vowels and consonants that all ran together.

As Bob, who managed to capture the whole thing, later said, it was like "some mystical language" only the horse could appreciate. From a spooked animal, Solar Gold became wonderfully self-possessed. All need to blow off steam was quite forgotten.

"Say, that was fantastic!" the girl strapper told Chloe, sounding amazed and embarrassed. She moved to resume Solar Gold's reins. "You obviously know a lot about horses."

Chloe permitted herself a smile though she was feeling a little strange. "I was the proud owner of a pony by the time I was six," she confessed.

"Go on." The strapper started to say something but changed her mind. It would take a lifetime to learn the line of patter Chloe Cavanagh had used. Whatever it *meant*.

"I'm going to make sure this makes the papers tomorrow," Bob crowed. "That's if I managed to get the shot at all." He grinned, harking back to the koala rally.

Gabriel, when he heard, all but ran to the ring. A colleague from one of the other stations had filled him in.

"I've never seen anything like it in my life, Gabe," his friend said with a silly grin. "Chloe hasn't changed much, has she? Always in the thick of it. Personally, I'd be a bit worried about her if I were you. She might want to take over your job. Next Sir Llew."

Gabriel, full of personal anxiety, couldn't agree more. Chloe's guardian angel was as impetuous as she was.

When Chloe saw Gabriel rushing towards her, a sweet grateful smile appeared on her face. "Oh, Gabriel," she said, and let him take her protectively in his arms in a wonderful hug.

"Chloe." His breath rasped. "I've decided it's time to take you home. I'm not even willing to turn my back on you for a moment."

"I'm fine, fine. Don't worry," Chloe murmured, and then came as close as she had ever done in her life to fainting.

The doctor made her lie quietly for a time. "Does she often do this sort of thing?" he asked Gabe.

"Only in emergencies," Chloe piped up, lifting her head from the small pillow.

"I told you to be quiet, young lady," Doctor Fraser admonished her. "I'm very interested to find out what exactly happened. Even run a few tests. Everything seems perfectly normal but she's acting as though she's been pushed hard. Too much excitement, I suppose. It has that effect."

"There's nothing wrong with me," Chloe said, and certainly looked it. "Gabriel insisted we stop to see you."

"I'm sure Gabe did the right thing," Doctor Fraser, who was Gabriel's own doctor, replied. "On your own admission, you almost fainted."

"Well, I feel terrific now," Chloe said, and she did. The peculiar languidness had left her, the tingly sensation in her body like an overload of electricity. She felt full of vitality. Her eyes were sapphire bright and there was a lovely natural pink in her cheeks.

"I'll keep a sharp watch on her," Gabriel promised.

"All right. You're welcome to see me again," Doctor

Fraser said as he walked them to the door. "Gabe, it must be time for your yearly check-up?"

"I'll be in touch," Gabe promised, desperate to get Chloe alone.

"Why don't we call in at my place first?" he suggested rather tautly as they pulled away from the surgery. The incident at the racecourse had brought home to him how essential Chloe was to his very existence. It was all part of the ecstasy and the terror of loving. "I want to talk to you and we're almost there."

Once in his apartment, Gabriel shut the door quickly, leading Chloe through to the living room. It emanated the sort of dynamic male elegance he had himself, Chloe thought. It was a very masculine apartment, the furnishings and the artworks making strong statements. Reflecting Gabriel's personality. She watched him strip off the formal jacket he had worn with so much dash, loosening his silk tie. Chloe took her own jacket off and hung it neatly over the back of a chair, adjusting the collar of her sleeveless vest. Then she turned and made herself as cosy as she could in the corner of one of the oversized burgundy leather sofas. She could sense Gabriel was off balance. She herself was unnerved by the tense current that glittered between them.

"What am I going to do about you?" Gabriel demanded without preamble.

"What do you *want* to do about me?" Her sweet smile flashed then faltered at something in his expression. Something that terrified her. A kind of wrenching pain. "You don't want to hurt me, Gabriel. Is that it? You can't bring yourself to tell me you're going away?"

"Lord, Chloe, you've decided that, have you?" He groaned, then sat down opposite her, enchanted by how she looked tucked into his large, clubby chair.

"Well, you did tell Tara." Chloe hadn't meant to say

that at all, only he was looking so handsome and arrogant.

"Did I, by Jove!" Gabriel's rugged face tautened, making him look very formidable.

Chloe bit her lip like a child. She picked up a rich brocade cushion and hugged it like it was protection. "All right, you didn't. I knew that in my bones. But no one is asking you to give up a wonderful opportunity, Gabriel, least of all me."

"Least of all you," he scoffed, throwing up his hands. "Don't talk like a little fool, Chloe. You're very important to me. You have needs that have to be met. Demands you can make on me. Let it out."

It would be wonderful if she could but, incredibly, she was fighting to keep it in.

All too aware of it, Gabriel abruptly stood up, moved across to her and took the cushion out of her arms. "What's this, another defence?" He let his fingers slide down her satiny cheek, feeling the consuming fire start up inside him. "You're hurting, aren't you, and you don't know what to do about it?"

Her whole body was responding to his touch. Little pulses flicking here, flicking there, drumming in time to the high beat of her heart.

"Try and understand me, Gabriel. I haven't had a good life."

"That's all changed, Chloe." He stroked her hair away from her face.

"Has it?" She let out a long, shuddering sigh. "Are you going?" she demanded.

"Its pretty clear you wouldn't come with me," he said.

"No, my mother needs care, Gabriel, you see."

"Chloe, your mother isn't sick anymore. I feel that very strongly. You've been there for her through thick and thin. Now she's home, gaining in strength every day.

I'm here for you in any capacity—friend, supporter, provider, protector, anything you want—but you have to take responsibility for your feelings.''

"What, pack my bags and come with you to New York?" Chloe flared.

"I don't believe I said I was going anywhere," he drawled. "On the other hand, I can see you're quite willing to let me go."

She hung her head, her breath strangely in her throat. "Gabriel, don't do this to me. If you went away, I'd be lonely all my life."

"How lonely?" he asked bluntly, as if doubting her declaration.

"I couldn't change back to what I was. You've been my teacher. You've filled my life even when I didn't want to give my heart away, when I didn't want to place my trust in you."

"So what's changed?" he asked laconically. "Oh, hell." He pulled her across his knees. "Why am I putting you through this? I guess wild horses wouldn't drag it out of you."

For a heart-stopping moment she stared into his eyes. "You want me to tell you I love you, or what?"

"Don't you think it might be a good idea?" he suggested dryly.

"All right, I love you, totally, completely," she said fiercely. "Does that satisfy you?"

"No." He shook his dark head. "Would you marry me tomorrow? No, don't take time off to think up a good excuse. Just answer from the heart."

"Gabriel." She covered her face in shock, confusion and a frantic joy. "If you don't stop teasing you'll drive me really crazy."

"That's the intention, now answer."

She lay back in his arms, her dilemma in her eyes.

"I'd do anything. I adore you. But I can't hurt my mother."

He bent, kissing her hard. "As if I'd want you to."

"But I can't bind you to me in this way, Gabriel," she agonised. "I love you. I want the best of everything for you."

"Why would you think I wouldn't have the best of everything in *you?*" he responded. "One of the things that makes you so beautiful is your sense of loyalty. Your sense of family. I never had a family, Chloe. It was the tragedy of *my* life. *I'm certain* we can make a family together. However ambitious I might be, I can satisfy my goals right here."

"You do mean that?" she begged. "You're not just saying it because it's what I want to hear?"

"Chloe, I've already told my American friends I'm home to stay," he said easily. "*Home.* Doesn't that say it all? The most important thing in the world to me is how much I love you and how much you love me back. Power and possessions don't define what I want from life. I want to be successful, sure, but more than anything I want a wife I adore. I want children to love and enjoy."

"How many?" she tried to joke but it didn't quite come off. "It does have *something* to do with me."

"Two or three, okay?" He dropped another kiss on her mouth. "I want to love and protect them until they're ready to take on the world. Is it too much to want, Chloe?"

"It's the same thing I want," she said, an answering profound feeling in her eyes.

"So you're going to marry me, after all?"

"Oh, yes, darling." Her arms lifted, tightening around his neck. "I can't think of anything more wonderful."

"You're not going to make me wait long?" His black eyes burned with infinite desire.

"No, darling."

Chloe really didn't know why but as she slipped down into Gabriel's passionate embrace, she felt like wings were closing over their heads. Wings that enfolded them in a shining cocoon.

Why not? Love is a very special kind of magic.

HEAVEN

Mr. Bliss chose that same day to voice his concerns about young Titus with Lucas. Chloe's birth guardian angel was well and truly on the mend and looking much more like his ancient splendid self.

"It's not that Titus hasn't brought great joy into Chloe's life," Mr. Bliss said, "which is highly commendable. But like all youngsters he's impulsive. For instance, just today he directed far too much energy into Chloe's body. Not intentionally, of course. Simply doesn't know the strength of his own powers."

"Exactly, Mr. Bliss," Lucas sighed. "As they say, one can't put an old head on young shoulders."

"You do realise he was Chloe's little brother in the other life?"

"Well, I never!" Lucas flapped his wings in astonishment, then tucked them neatly back again. "Surely this sort of thing doesn't happen often?"

"Rarely, very rarely." Mr. Bliss made one of his beautiful prayful gestures. "But it has all turned out terribly well. As I say, Titus has been of great service to his mother and Chloe. In fact he's been working overtime. I'm thinking very seriously of awarding him his three-quarter wings."

Lucas responded with a smile full of loving kindness.

"He'll be thrilled. What it is to be so young and vigorous!"

Mr. Bliss laughed and nodded. "You, of course, will be returning to your given charge, Lucas." His brilliant dark eyes crinkled. "We're all so pleased you're back to your old self and the wing is functioning perfectly. It will be easier for you, too, now that Chloe has found her nice Gabriel."

"Even we angels can do with a little bit of help," Lucas said with great good cheer. "And Titus, have you anything in mind for him, Mr. Bliss?"

"Exactly the same question I've been asking myself." Mr. Bliss drew his fingertips together. "I see Titus as a guiding star," he said very pensively. "Really, I should be thinking of placing him with a baby."

EPILOGUE

CHLOE was always to remember her son's birth as a time of white light. The blazing white lights of the city, the lights from the other cars as Gabriel raced her to the hospital—she was early by two weeks. There were more lights at the hospital entrance, at reception, the brightest dazzle in the delivery room where she was taken, great radiant orbs. She remembered the tremendous sense of urgency. The hospital staff bustling around her. Gabriel's dark golden face almost as pale as hers with anxiety. She remembered his warm strong hand as it held on to hers for dear life. Finally a nursing sister had to prise them apart.

She remembered a nurses's voice telling her very earnestly to breathe deeply.

"That's it, dear, breathe in, hold it, relax."

How *could* she when the pain kept coming for her? Until finally, miraculously, she needed no one to tell her what to do.

Her son wanted to be born. She heard his first triumphant cry.

Here I am!

That was when the heavens opened, pouring forth their glory.

When they put him in her arms she thought her heart couldn't hold all the joy that was in her. Her marriage to Gabriel had brought such happiness. She had thought her cup had spilleth over. Now this. This adorable little bundle, perfect in every respect from the soft silky down on his head—dark like Gabriel's—to his wonderful little toes, with their tiny perfect pearl nails.

She kissed him. *Kissed* him, exulting in his entrancing baby's smell.

My son!

The sister who was with her bent over the bed beaming her delight at a safe, beautiful delivery. "You've got a little angel there, Mrs. McGuire, and no mistake!"

"Haven't I." She smiled radiantly, her face Madonna-like in its love and pride.

The following day the family returned; Gabriel, a new father, walking on air, Delia with a wonderful bloom on her, thrilled at being a grandmother, Janet, Gabriel's mother who had flown to the mainland especially for the birth and was staying with Delia with whom she had formed an instant rapport, all of them transported with joy and a great sense of hope for the future.

Gabriel took his baby son in his strong arms, an endearing sight, he being such a big man and the baby so tiny. "He's absolutely perfect, isn't he?" he breathed with reverence. "Our own miracle of love."

"He's that!" Both grandmothers came to stand at Gabriel's shoulder, their faces soft and beautiful with shared joy. "So what are you going to call him, my darlings?" Delia asked, entranced her little grandchild was actually clinging to her finger.

Gabriel's brilliant eyes rested lovingly on his wife, his treasure. "I thought maybe Michael?" He waited for her all-important approval, but his beloved Chloe was staring at some point over his shoulder. Her lovely face was filled with such wonderment she might have discovered the secret of the universe; her cheeks filled with the soft pink of a blossoming camellia as if she had absorbed the beauty of the flower. How he loved her. His wife, now the mother of this wonderful tiny bundle.

Behind the family tableau Chloe continued to focus on the shimmering image that was slowly beginning to materialise.

An angel! Michael's guardian angel. The knowledge penetrated like a shaft of heavenly light. The angel was bending close, looking down on the baby with a smile of such tender radiance Chloe felt her heart melt.

"Timmy?" she whispered, as full knowledge descended on her. "Is it really you?" It had to be. She had never seen anyone look so much like herself. Hair, eyes, features, but she could never attain such…such…*glory!*

The angel hung suspended a moment more, poised over the baby, such a small angel to have such *splendid* wings! They enclosed the family group.

So attuned to his wife, Gabriel moved back to the bedside, certain something important was happening to her.

"Darling?" he questioned, willing her back to him.

Smilingly, she reached up to take his hand, on her face an expression of such joy she was shining. "Michael! Of course. I love it already. After all, we do have a tradition of angels in the family."

In 1999 in Harlequin Romance® marriage is top of the agenda!

Get ready for a great new series by some of our most popular authors, bringing romance to the workplace! This series features gorgeous heroes and lively heroines who discover that mixing business with pleasure can lead to anything...even matrimony!

Books in this series are:

January 1999
Agenda: Attraction! by Jessica Steele

February 1999
Boardroom Proposal by Margaret Way

March 1999
Temporary Engagement by Jessica Hart

April 1999
Beauty and the Boss by Lucy Gordon

May 1999
The Boss and the Baby by Leigh Michaels

From boardroom...to bride and groom!

Available wherever Harlequin books are sold.

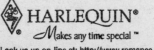

HARLEQUIN®
Makes any time special ™

Question: How do you find the sexy cowboy of your dreams?

Answer: Read on....

Texas Grooms Wanted!
is a brand-new miniseries from

Harlequin Romance®

Meet three very special heroines who are all looking for very special Texas men—their future husbands! Good men may be hard to find, but these women have experts on hand. They've all signed up with the Yellow Rose Matchmakers. The oldest and the best matchmaking service in San Antonio, Texas, the Yellow Rose guarantees to find any woman her perfect partner....

So for the cutest cowboys in the whole state of Texas, look out for:

HAND-PICKED HUSBAND
by Heather MacAllister in January 1999

BACHELOR AVAILABLE!
by Ruth Jean Dale in February 1999

THE NINE-DOLLAR DADDY
by Day Leclaire in March 1999

TEXAS GROOMS WANTED!

Only cowboys need apply...

Available wherever
Harlequin Romance books
are sold.

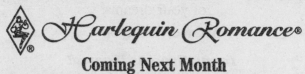

Harlequin Romance®

Coming Next Month

In January look out for a brand-new trilogy featuring the cutest cowboys in the whole state of Texas:

#3535 HAND-PICKED HUSBAND Heather MacAllister
The whole state of Texas seems convinced that Autumn Reese was born to be Clayton Barnett's bride. The whole state bar Clay and Autumn, that is. Which is why she and Clay have dared each other to sign up at the Yellow Rose Matchmakers. Only, watching Clay date other women has made Autumn realize that perhaps her Mr. Right might just be the one she's had within her grasp all along....

Texas Grooms Wanted! is a brand-new trilogy in Harlequin Romance®. Meet three heroines who are all looking for very special Texas men—their future husbands!

Texas Grooms Wanted!: *Only cowboys need apply!*

Also starting in January, find out what happens after office hours in:

#3536 AGENDA: ATTRACTION! Jessica Steele
Edney had been grateful when a handsome stranger had saved her from the unwanted attentions of another man—and amazed when that stranger had kissed her and asked her out to dinner! But Saville Craythorne was not amused. He'd discovered that his new PA was the girl he'd rescued—and he *never* mixed business with pleasure!

Marrying the Boss–*When marriage is top of the agenda!*

#3537 ONLY BY CHANCE Betty Neels
Henrietta's life hadn't been easy. Then, with the help of consultant neurosurgeon Mr. Adam Ross-Pitt, her small world changed irrevocably. He was, of course, far beyond her reach, and if her gratitude to him tipped into love, there was no need for him to know—even if he did keep coming to her rescue!

#3538 MAKE-BELIEVE MOTHER Pamela Bauer and Judy Kaye
Bryan Shepard wanted a mother, and new neighbor Alexis Gordon was perfect for the job. He just had to convince his dad she'd make the perfect wife....

Kids & Kisses—*Where kids and kisses go hand in hand!*